BEST GAY ROMANCE 2014

BEST GAY ROMANCE 2014

Edited by

TIMOTHY J. LAMBERT

AND R. D. COCHRANE

Published in the United States by Cleis Press, Inc.,
2246 Sixth Street, Berkeley, California 94710.

Printed in the United States.
Cover design: Scott Idleman/Blink
Cover photograph: Bart Geerligs/Getty Images
Text design: Frank Wiedemann

First Edition.
10 9 8 7 6 5 4 3 2 1

Trade paper ISBN: 978-1-62778-011-7
E-book ISBN: 978-1-62778-024-7

For Richard Labonté

CONTENTS

ix Introduction • Timothy J. Lambert

1 Strange Propositions • Eric Gober
18 My Adventure with Tom Sawyer • Jameson Currier
35 True In My Fashion • Paul Brownsey
45 Sight • Jordan Taylor
67 Falling • James Booth
73 Thanksgiving • Shawn Anniston
83 The Invincible Theatre • Felice Picano
102 Carver Comes Home • Rob Byrnes
121 Spill Your Troubles on Me, Love • Georgina Li
128 Quality Time • Lewis DeSimone
151 Brooding Intervals • Kevin Langson
163 Dandelions • Tony Calvert
179 Shep: A Dog • Alex Jeffers
197 There's No Question It's Love • N. S. Beranek
202 Save the Last Dance for Me • David Puterbaugh

213 Afterword • R. D. Cochrane

215 About the Authors
219 About the Editors

INTRODUCTION

I had a different idea about romance when I was young than I do now. I blame it on prom. The American tradition of prom, for the benefit of readers outside of the United States, is a dance for high school students usually held before graduation. Because it's a formal event, expectations are high. Luckily, because I was gay, my expectations were low. Yes, I had to look presentable in my rented tuxedo and show my date a good time, but she was a good friend and knew a hotel room wasn't on our agenda. Plus, she knew that I'd slept with her brother.

We had a great time. We went out to dinner with friends, made an appearance at the prom and danced, had photos taken, and then we all went to my date's house where I walked into a surprise party since it was also my birthday that weekend. It was a magical evening. Everybody was dressed up and having fun, and the night was suddenly all about me.

The bar was set very high for magical moments. In my superficial twenties, I loved it when my date took us to the perfect restaurant, whisked us away for a magical weekend out of town or got us into an exclusive party. An exotic arrangement of flowers with a note meant I was on his mind. How wonderful! Pointing out something I liked in a shop window and having him buy it for me on the spot: unexpected and rewarding!

Luckily, I mellowed and learned to appreciate simpler things: a quiet walk together on a beach or in a park, a night at the symphony or even a well-expressed compliment.

As I find myself in what one might refer to as middle age, I realize romance isn't tangible. While doing seated dumbbell press sets in the gym yesterday I was watching myself in the mirror to make sure my form was correct, and I noticed a guy at the preacher curl bench behind me. He was an adorable blond with icy blue eyes, a Paul Walker and Brad Pitt hybrid. Like me, he was listening to music through earbuds while he worked out. Whatever he was listening to was making him laugh periodically. His set jaw and determined veneer would crack, replaced by a toothy smile and a radiance normally reserved for golden tapestries.

I watched him and thought, *Heaven would be spending the rest of my days thinking of ways to make him smile like that again and again.* Getting up and asking him what he was listening to was an obvious conversation starter. But did I do it?

The best part of romance, in my opinion, is what might happen next. The grand gestures, fanciful planning or glittering prizes are merely vehicles to help us arrive at that pivotal moment where we stop and realize, *This is wonderful. Now what? Whatever it is, we're in it together.*

There's nothing more romantic than the realization that anything is possible.

Timothy J. Lambert

STRANGE PROPOSITIONS

Eric Gober

While Jess cruised the cool walkway between the Cinerama Dome and 24 Hour Fitness, I worked noisy Sunset Boulevard. A horn honked, punctuating my frustration. We needed males under thirty, but it was slim pickings this morning. I scanned the intersection at Vine. Among the women and dudes over thirty crossing the street, I spotted a lean guy in a Dodgers cap. I shielded my eyes from sun glare and squinted. Nope. He was just outside the limit, probably thirty-one. Didn't matter. I knew his type. Even if he were twenty-four, he'd have said no. The guy with the Ray-Bans and trimmed beard, on the other hand, would likely say yes. But he was way too old, at least thirty-four. The blond in the UCLA shirt, however, was perfect, not a day over twenty-two. But I didn't even try to go after him. He didn't look the least bit interested in romance. He'd have scoffed at my proposition.

"Jackpot, Kenny!" Jess click-clacked up the sidewalk, all smiles, waving her clipboard. "I nailed seven guys in a row coming out of the gym."

"You mean the quota's filled?"

"Yep." She beamed.

I shook my head in amazement. How'd she do it? Romantic comedies were always a hard sell to males under thirty. However, tonight's film was downright impossible—a deadpan love story about seniors. Yet thanks to Jess, seven guys in my age bracket would sit among folks our parents' age, yawn through a grainy rough cut and exact their revenge afterward when they filled out questionnaires. If the film was mediocre, their votes would seal its fate. *Penelope's Proposal* would go straight to video with no coveted theatrical release.

She planted a hand on her hip. "Now tell me what happened with Trevor."

I'd insisted we finish recruiting before I told her about the phone call, but I still wasn't ready to spill the beans. "Let's re-caffeinate first."

She rolled her pretty green eyes at me. "Fine, leave me in suspense till I die."

We trekked up the boulevard to Groundwork Coffee, our go-to place for espresso whenever we recruited audiences at the Arclight theaters. I was trying to woo Trevor to L.A. He'd refused to leave Wichita in May when Movie Research Group hired me. I was thrilled to move on from my first job out of college—recruiting shoppers for focus groups at Towne East Mall—and was ready to experience a place more exciting than my native Kansas. But Trevor wanted no part of weird California. He was content to live in a world where by day he and I masqueraded as buddies. Only in the evenings did we strip off our masks and love one another properly for a few hours inside my apartment before he returned to his family's ranch south of town. I needed more from life, but I also needed him.

Now my mission was selling him on L.A. I didn't tout star

sightings at glamorous restaurants, sun-bronzed hunks in BMWs and Mercedes, or sparkling pool parties in the Hollywood Hills. I sought the familiar, and L.A. delivered plain tract homes in Northridge, modest horse ranches in Sunland and ordinary parishioners at a Methodist church in Canoga Park. I steered clear of anything overtly gay whenever we talked on the phone. I didn't mention the extravagant Pride parade in West Hollywood that Jess took me to in June, or her older brother's wedding in September at a Santa Barbara winery where he'd married his boyfriend now that same-sex marriage was legal in California. I didn't want to spook Trevor, and my approach seemed to be paying off.

Jess and I settled at a high table and sipped our lattes.

"Well?"

"He said five months apart has worn him down. He's coming to L.A."

"Yay! When's he moving?"

"He'll be here for Thanksgiving." I braced myself for her reaction. "But only for a visit."

She smacked the tabletop so hard her wooden bracelet clacked. "Ah poo, you need to get him to move out here before the election and marry his behind. The polling numbers are looking bad on Prop 8."

"Jess, I told you I'll never get Trevor to walk down the aisle with me."

"What's the matter with him?"

"He's just old fashioned. I don't mind that."

"You guys are really selling yourselves short." She shook her head. "Maybe in time he'll change."

"I can always hope. Right now though, I just want him to miss me so much he moves out here. Will you help me plan an old-fashioned Thanksgiving dinner for him?"

"Of course, love. I just want more for you, that's all."

"I know. Me, too. But with Trevor I gotta take what I can get."

I felt someone hovering as I unzipped the pup tent's door flap and poked my head inside. I was at Target in West Hollywood examining gear because I wanted to take Trevor camping in the Angeles National Forest. Nothing turned him on more than the two of us getting naked in a sleeping bag under the stars.

I extricated myself from the tiny tent and was momentarily startled. A drag queen in a pink satin jumpsuit and platform heels towered over me and batted inch-long false eyelashes. Trapped in her ratted brunette wig were shiny golden stars, two sparkly silver comets, and an iridescent-pink Saturn. She pointed at me with a hot-pink false fingernail. "You were in *Borat*, weren't you, honey?"

"No, sorry, I wasn't."

"Are you sure? No, wait. You were in *Jackass Number Two*, right?"

"I think you've got me confused with someone else."

"No, you're somebody; I'm sure of it. I know a strange star when I see one. Your kind's not like the rising stars, falling stars and red-hot supergiants orbiting Planet Hollywood. You don't give a damn if paparazzi catch you shopping at Target."

"Seriously, I just recently moved here from Wichita."

"By yourself? That makes you an orphan planet, honey, captured by Hollywood's gravitational pull. Have you attracted a lovely moon yet to orbit and adore you?"

"Not exactly."

"Well, let me help you fix that." She extended her hand and firmly shook mine. "I'm Venus the Fly Trap."

"I'm Kenny."

"I want you to catch my show tonight at Fubar. The place ain't the brightest sector in the constellation we call Southern California, but it's interesting. My *Age of Aquarius* show draws every kind to that little black hole in the wall—sexy dark nebulae, cute rogue planets and a brown dwarf who loves to moon everyone. You're bound to hit it off with somebody."

I liked her. She seemed genuinely friendly, and she was outrageously brave. I could never get up the nerve to dress like that, even in private. I was tempted to go, but then I thought of Trevor. "Sorry, Venus, I gotta take a rain check."

"Fine, but I'll be expecting you sometime soon. Don't stand me up." She winked good-bye with her long dark lashes and retreated from the camping display.

Universal City normally yielded an easy, done-by-three-P.M. harvest. However, Jess called me that morning, coughed up a pint of phlegm and wheezed that she looked greener than a witch's wart. I told her to stay home and not worry. I'd recruit tonight's screening myself. No one would ever know she wasn't on the clock. But now it was five P.M., and I was running out of time. Predictably, I'd skewed sampling toward females, and I was desperate to nail a young male. Otherwise, I'd get Jess and myself both fired. So for the hundredth time, I traversed the crowded stretch between Hard Rock's gigantic flaming guitar and the humongous blue gorilla scaling CityWalk's neon sign. A movie shoot was wrapping up inside Bubba Gump Shrimp Co. I surveyed the horde of tourists staring into windows trying to catch a glimpse of a star.

"Excuse me, bud."

I turned around and looked straight into the face of a breathtaking dude. His blue eyes, fair skin and cropped dark hair had to be the product of a long line of gorgeous Irishmen.

"Can I squeeze through?"

I stepped aside and he brushed past me carrying a plunger and a can of Drano.

Don't let him get away, you fool.

I waved my clipboard and blurted, "You feel like seeing a movie tonight?"

He stopped and looked at me curiously. "You wanna go on a date with me?"

"Um—what I meant was do you want to attend a screening tonight? It's free. All you have to do is fill out a questionnaire afterward."

"You going?"

"No, it's off limits to me."

"What's it about?"

"A fading star who falls in love with her young plastic surgeon."

"Sounds like a piece of Hollywood crap."

I shrugged sheepishly. "Well, your answers to the questionnaire could help flush it down the Hollywood tidy bowl."

He grinned and I wanted to melt. He had gorgeous, even white teeth. "All right, I'll go, but you owe me one."

"Great." I fished a pen from my pocket and steadied my clipboard. "What's your name?"

"Nate Murphy."

"Age?"

"Twenty-eight."

"Perfect, exactly the age I need. What's your occupation?"

"Murphy!" someone yelled. The production crew was exiting Bubba Gump. "It's a wrap. Time for a beer!"

Nate waved the plunger at them. "Not tonight!"

My heart sank. I was going to have to exclude him. "People in the business can't attend the screening, sorry."

"But don't you need me, bud, to fill your quota?"

"Oh man, you *really* know too much about the biz to attend."

He shook the can of Drano. "All I know right now is I have to unclog a drain."

He stepped close to me and spoke softly into my ear. "Write down plumber. You won't be telling a lie, and you won't be sorry if I attend, either." His breath on my skin made me shudder. I wanted to lean into him and feel his lips on my neck. Instead, I scrawled *plumber* on my recruiting sheet.

"If they ask, tell them you're a wiz with pipes and crescent wrenches."

"I will. Cross my heart."

"Awesome, screening's at seven o'clock at the AMC Theaters right over there. Just tell them your name, and you're in."

"Aren't you going to ask me for my phone number? Or do I have to ask for yours?"

I was tempted to rattle mine off, but then I thought of Trevor. "No, give me yours."

"Will you call?"

"Definitely," I said, certain that I wouldn't and disappointed that it had to be that way.

I was caged again in my chicken coop of an apartment, cramped on the love seat and watching a TV commercial. Mr. T berated a swishy speed walker, who bore an uncanny resemblance to me, calling him "a disgrace to the man race" and pelting him with Snickers bars until he ran away. The commercial ended, and special election-night news coverage by NBC's local affiliate returned. I grabbed the remote and pressed MUTE. I didn't want to hear the update. Gone was the happiness I'd felt when California turned blue on the electoral map and gave Democrats the White House. Numbers were coming in now on California's ballot propositions. With each update, Proposition 8 pulled farther ahead. Jess had been right. It was going to pass. I wished Trevor were sitting next to me. I wouldn't feel quite so blue.

My flip phone rang—it was him. I knew he wasn't calling to talk about our president-elect. He was apolitical. He had to be either horny or lonely.

"Hey, what're you doing up so late?" I asked.

"Can't sleep."

"You wanna have phone sex?"

"Not tonight."

Perfect, he was lonely—tonight we'd be on the same emotional page.

"I can't wait for you to get here. I bought a tent and a sleeping bag for us to go camping in the mountains. There are secluded spots along a river—"

"Kenny, I'm not coming for Thanksgiving."

"Oh c'mon, why not?" There was a long pause. "Trevor? Are you there?"

"I'm seeing someone new."

"What! Since when?"

"September."

"But last week when we talked, you said you loved *me*!"

"I told you when you left Kansas there were no guarantees."

"You also told me you didn't want to break up."

"Because I hoped you'd move back. But I finally gave up on you in August."

"Thanks a lot for letting me know."

"You know I'd rather be with you than anyone. If you come home, I'll break it off with him. It'll be just you and me again."

"For two hours a night, two times a week?"

"Don't exaggerate."

"I'm not!"

"C'mon, you know I need to be discreet."

"Well, I don't want to be!"

He sighed. "I don't even know you anymore, man. California's ruined you."

"No, California's opening my eyes. Ever since I got here, I've done nothing but hole up in my apartment every night and pine for you the way I did in Wichita. What a damn fool. I'm not doing that anymore."

"Suit yourself," he said and hung up on me.

I snapped my phone shut, threw it across the room and unmuted the TV.

"We have a projection to make," said a talking head. "Proposition 2 will pass, giving farm animals the right not to be inhumanely confined. Other closely watched ballot measures remain too close to call. But with new precincts reporting, Proposition 8, which revokes gays' and lesbians' right to marry, inches closer to passage."

What the hell was the matter with people? How could you vote to treat animals humanely but not fellow human beings? I'd go mad if I sat here and watched that hateful proposition become law. And no way was I staying cooped up thinking about Trevor all night.

I turned off the TV, grabbed my keys and headed for Santa Monica Boulevard.

Fubar, I discovered, was a dim hole in the wall on the not-so-glamorous side of West Hollywood. I didn't care. I was glad to be out. I ordered a cosmopolitan, meandered toward the stage and sipped my drink.

"Let's all bow our heads and say a little prayer," Venus the

Fly Trap intoned. Tonight she'd donned curly blonde locks and a yellow Bo-Peep dress. "Dear Sweet Jesus, may the people of California have the good sense to do the right thing and say yes to marriage equality. Amen."

"Do you always pray in bars, Venus?" asked the dwarf on stage with her.

"Yes, Brownie, I do, and I never go to church without a good bottle of gin."

I laughed so hard she looked in my direction. Her face lit up like a jeweled star atop a Christmas tree.

"Friends of Dorothy, we have a guest here tonight from Wichita, Kansas. Hi, honey!" She waved, and when I raised my glass to her, a spotlight shined on me. "Thanks for coming." She beamed.

"Come again and again and again," Brownie said, making jerk-off motions with his hand.

The spotlight disappeared, and I sucked down my drink. As I returned to the bar to order another, someone grabbed my arm. "It *is* you."

I turned and looked right into the face of Nate the plumber. He'd grown a dark and sexy five-o'clock shadow.

"Hey," I said stupidly.

"I'm still waiting for your call, bud."

Oh god, how was I going to maneuver out of this? I decided to tell the truth. "I didn't call because I was involved with someone else. But that ended tonight. How about if I give you my number? That way you can call me."

"How about I get even with you and throw it away?"

"Fair enough, but I'm still gonna give it to you."

He let go of my arm and smiled. "Maybe I'll forgive you, instead."

"I'd really like that."

He took out his phone and entered my digits as I rattled them off.

"So how was the screening?"

"Really good, actually. I'm glad you talked me into going. I'm a sucker for romance on the big screen."

"Me, too—I guess because there's so little in real life."

"Murphy!" someone yelled from across the bar. "Let's go!"

"I have to be on set early tomorrow. How about if I call you, and we do something Saturday?"

"Sure."

He gave me a look. "You're not going to blow me off again, are you?"

"No, never again."

"Cross your heart?"

When I crossed my heart, his smile was gorgeous.

"All right, see you this weekend."

He left me at the bar, and I decided against ordering another drink. I suddenly didn't feel like I had all that much sorrow to drown.

As I walked to the door, Venus lip-synched "Bleeding Love." When I waved good-bye, she grabbed the fabric of her Bo-Peep skirt, tipped her head at me and curtseyed.

Our trek had started on Beachwood Drive, with the HOLLYWOOD sign sitting on the mountain ahead, grinning at us. We'd wound through a land of storybook cottages and castles and hiked up steep green slopes. Now we were atop the mountain, grinning at the sign's backside.

"L.A. looks like a giant chessboard from here," I said. "That tall skyscraper downtown is a queen."

"I've always thought that." Nate pointed out the city's other skyscrapers. "She's surrounded by shining knights and rooks.

She and her army want to march rightward, capture all those pawns in the middle and take down those two dark bishops by Fox Studios."

I couldn't help but smile at him. I was liking the way he saw the world. Unlike Trevor, he had an imagination. Must have come from working in the business. He'd confessed midway up the mountain that he wasn't a plumber but a property master. I'd marveled at his ingenuity when he told me about a sci-fi fantasy production he'd worked on that had almost no budget. He'd created talking books, magic wands, cosmic ray guns, and feathered druid staffs from sale items he'd found at Kmart and Home Depot.

"What are you doing tomorrow evening?" he asked.

"No plans."

"There's a demonstration against Prop 8 in Silver Lake. You wanna go with me?"

I wasn't really comfortable with the idea of attending a protest. It seemed so radical. However, I detested Proposition 8. "Okay, sure. I still can't believe Californians gave rights to chickens and took them away from human beings."

Now he smiled at me. "I've got a wild idea."

"Uh-oh."

"C'mon, let's hit Hollywood Boulevard."

Lassie, Lucille Ball, Alfred Hitchcock, W.C. Fields—I still had a hard time walking Hollywood Boulevard without looking down to read the golden names etched into pink stars. At Fleetwood Mac's, Nate grabbed my hand.

"Let's go in here." He led me toward a blue-and-gold art deco building with a neon sign blinking HOLLYWOOD TOYS & COSTUMES.

Inside was a prop master's paradise. Nate slowed to eye cases displaying faux gangsta bling and fake Crown Jewels. I couldn't believe he was brave enough to be holding my hand in public. Or that I had nerve enough to let him.

"C'mon, the suspense is killing me," I said. "Are we shopping for a movie shoot?"

"Nope," he said, resuming his mission through this world of fantasy. He tugged me through an arsenal of plastic weapons and past shelves of outlandish hats, spooky skulls and creepy rubber masks. He guided us around carousels of bright makeup and styled wigs, and we sidestepped bins filled with all sorts of plastic tchotchkes. He finally stopped and let go of my hand near a wall lined with packaged costumes.

"I have a proposal for you."

"But it's too soon—and too late—for us to get married," I joked.

He smiled. "Bud, I like the way your mind works. I think I'm really gonna like getting to know you."

"Same here."

"I've been thinking about chickens since we were on the mountain. I bet they're thankful for gays like us who voted to support their rights. I bet they'd support our rights if they could."

I was thankful Trevor wasn't here listening to him. He'd say chickens are the stupidest animals on earth and call Nate a fool. I said, "You're probably right."

He reached for a package stuffed with fuzzy bright yellow material. Then he grabbed another and handed it to me. I eyed the label. It was a chicken suit.

"What do you say we represent those thankful chickens at the protest in Silver Lake?"

When I tried imagining myself in that big yellow costume, weirdness grabbed hold of me. I wouldn't blend into the crowd tomorrow. Thousands of staring eyes would be upon me as I marched through Sunset Junction. Suddenly, all the strange things in the costume shop began closing in on me. I quickly hung the package back on the wall. "I'm afraid I'm going to have to pass."

"Why?"

"I just can't do it."

I expected him to be disappointed with me and that I'd recoil at his dissatisfaction. I thought a chasm would open up between us, and I'd watch him and his strange world immediately float away.

Instead, he gazed at me, seeking my approval. "Do you mind if I wear one?"

Trevor had never sought my approval, and he wouldn't be caught dead with Nate in or out of a chicken suit.

"Doesn't matter what you wear tomorrow," I said, taking his hand, "as long as we're together."

For once, Jess didn't have to hard sell me into meeting her on La Brea Avenue and standing in the ridiculous, hour-long line at Pink's Hot Dogs, because I was itching to tell her about my morning with Nate and how much I liked him.

"Remember when we recruited parents to bring their kids to the Sherman Oaks Galleria for that traveling circus movie?" I asked.

"What a nightmare that was."

"Nate was the clown all the kids loved."

"The one with the water balloon animals?"

"Yep, they were so difficult to handle the director yelled at him, 'I don't give a flying rip if you're a prop master and don't know squat about acting. Get your ass into a clown suit and make sure no more of those fuckers pop.' So Nate suited up and stole the entire scene."

"Wow, he sounds just the opposite of Trevor."

"He is in so many ways. He asked a dozen questions about how you and I handle a movie recruit. Trevor never liked hearing about my market research work, even in Wichita when I recruited people for projects involving ranching."

We inched another step toward the ordering window. The smell of grilled onions made my empty stomach growl.

"Tomorrow we're going to a protest against Prop 8."

"That's kinda romantic."

"Yeah, but he wants to do something a little strange."

"What?"

"Dress up in a chicken suit."

"Prop 2-ers against Prop 8; that's genius! You should dress up with him."

"He wanted me to, but I told him no."

"Why?"

"I'd be too embarrassed."

"But no one's gonna know it's you."

"Maybe so...but still."

She fixed her pretty green eyes on me. "You need to rethink your answer to him, love. He's trying to include you in his life. That's more than Trevor was ever willing to do."

I parallel parked on Silver Lake Boulevard, cut the engine and stared at the chicken suit. Still in the package, it sat on the passenger seat with the receipt from my return visit to the costume shop. I tore it open, pulled out the head, and unflattened the rubbery yellow beak and bright red wattles and comb. I slipped the mask over my head and struggled to make it fit right. When I finally got the eyeholes positioned so I could see, I looked straight into the face of a straight dude. He was staring at me from the sidewalk like I was some kind of freak.

I couldn't do it. I pulled off the mask and tossed it on the floorboard.

I stepped out of my dusty blue Lumina and walked toward Marathon Street, where I was supposed to meet Nate. I spotted him on the corner. He was impossible to miss in the bright fuzzy fabric and orange rubber feet he wore. He held his mask in one hand and a large protest sign in the other. It read: U.S. CONSTITUTION: "ALL ANIMALS ARE EQUAL." PROP 8: "BUT SOME ANIMALS ARE MORE EQUAL THAN OTHERS." To my surprise, he looked far less comfortable being a huge yellow target than I thought he would. His look of relief when I waved touched my heart in a way Trevor never had.

A pickup truck revved and barreled by. My heart sank when it slowed and a dude leaned out the passenger-side window.

"Faggot!" he yelled, lobbing something at Nate.

Tires screeched and the jerks sped away.

I ran to the corner and discovered they'd pelted him with an egg. Yolk, white and flecks of shell dripped from his fuzzy yellow belly.

"Are you okay?"

"This wasn't a good idea," he said, sounding rattled.

"Let's get you cleaned up. I've got a beach towel in my car." I took the mask from him, grabbed his hand and led him to my Lumina. I opened the trunk, retrieved the towel and, as best as I could, wiped egg off his suit.

"Thank you," he said.

Right then, he looked so vulnerable I didn't care if I ended up with what was left of the egg on my T-shirt. I pulled him close and embraced his fuzzy yellow form. He gazed at me and smiled, and when his lips touched my neck, I remembered wanting him the day I recruited him outside Bubba Gump Shrimp Co.

Now my want was growing and growing.

I squeezed him tightly and then pulled away a little too fast.

He looked at me curiously as I hurried around the car and flung open the passenger door. I kicked off my shoes and stripped off my T-shirt.

"Wow, sexy," he said, flashing me his gorgeous grin. "But what exactly are you doing, bud?"

I grabbed the package off the car seat, ripped it wide open and slipped the bright yellow suit over my head. "I'm not about to let you face the world alone, my little chickadee."

MY ADVENTURE WITH TOM SAWYER

Jameson Currier

One of the best dates I ever had was not a date at all, or at least that was the way Evan reacted to it when I described my experience to him a few weeks after the fact. "Sounds like he was a cock tease," Evan said.

"No," I answered. "He was very sweet about everything."

The truth of the matter was that I had experienced a bad buildup before the great-date-that-was-not-really-a-date happened, which may have exaggerated my rating of it into the stratosphere. I had spent the prior year watching my love life turn me, literally, into one of the Great Walking Wounded. After breaking up with Tony I fought off a case of shingles; I went through two root canals while I was trying to decide whether or not to continue seeing Bernie after three months; and when the six-week relationship with Hal failed to go any further so did I, stumbling down a flight of steps and tearing a ligament in my foot, which required me to use a set of crutches in order to be mobile.

That was when Evan suggested I get out of town and do some healing. "Use the cabin," he said, referring to a small rural property he owned with his significant other. "We're not going up there again till next month."

It sounded like a plausible idea, even with crutches—to be isolated in the upstate woods without a guy anywhere in sight whom I could conceivably want to date, with no TV to watch and a bag of books to read—so Evan came to my apartment to drop off the cabin keys and I crawled aboard a bus and slept through the ride to the country. A few hours later, I was standing in a small, rural village wondering what I could possibly have been thinking by leaving behind my brand new air conditioner and round-the-clock support structure in the city. The taxicab I had called was not really a taxi nor a cab when it stopped in front of me to take me the next seven miles to the cabin, but the passenger seat in the front of an old red pickup truck, and the driver was not a fully licensed or registered or official or professional taxi driver either, but a boy, a late-teenaged boy with floppy golden hair, ice-blue eyes, an impossibly thin waist and the most beautiful set of arms that a slender young man could possess.

"My uncle's tied up at Mrs. Smith's farm," the young one said to me when he announced that he could be the only way I would get to my final destination. "You don't mind, do you? I can get you there in this."

Of course I was immediately suspicious—that was my urban reflex system cracking into high gear—and just as I was about to ask his age, I felt too old and vulnerable to move my mouth, standing there with my crutches and my suitcase of books, not able to take my eyes off of young Tom Sawyer's impossibly beautiful physique, and I was aware that I was having one of those awful motion-picture moments when the spinster realizes her tour guide is someone generations younger than she is. Or worse, finding myself in a country music version of *Death in Venice*.

(Did I mention that young Tom's shirt was sleeveless and unbuttoned in the front and that the jeans he wore were cutoffs because it was summer and it was hot? Should I mention that he had a baseball cap stuck in the back of the cutoffs and that even the slight bulge in the pocket that the hat created was unable to ruin the bubble shape of his ass? Would you believe me if I said the young man's complexion was pale and creamy except where it was red at the cheeks and slightly washed with freckles across the bridge of his nose and that his teeth were remarkably even and white, or is that taking the image too far?)

So hobble and humble myself I did, right into the front seat of his truck.

His name was Scott and his truck was a year older than he was. He was twenty. Almost. That meant he was still in his teens—nineteen, a teenager—and his truck was built the year I graduated college. I was old enough to be his father. I found this out as Scott drove and pointed out the local landmarks worth noting (the new Laundromat where the dryers took dollar bills, the green-painted barn on the property that had once been a women's commune, and the small stream and the new stone bridge where a wooden covered bridge had stood until a fire destroyed it three years before).

I was reluctant to confess too much about myself (sweeping the dirt under the rug, just like everyone in my family had always done), so I kept him talking about himself as much as I could. He had been laid off from his job on the assembly line at the window factory. The bad job market had meant cobbling together a series of odd jobs instead, such as helping his brother do landscaping work and filling in for his uncle with the car service. He managed to work in a few questions for me, too, asking where I lived in the city and how I had broken my foot. (Like a stupid old fool, I wanted to tell him: running after some guy who was running after someone else.)

As we drove up a mountainside, down into a valley and through a forest, he asked how long I was staying at the cabin. I answered a little less than a week, then found myself confessing my concerns about the wilderness around me like a true (and worried) cynical cosmopolitan: Were there bears and mice and snakes and mosquitoes and such out here? ("Well, yeah, yeah, yeah, and uh, yeah!") Was I likely to encounter them at the cabin? ("I think so. Maybe not all at the same time!") Would they play loud music like my upstairs neighbor and keep me up all night? ("Ah-huh. That sounds like my brother!")

He mentioned that his girlfriend's family was having a tough time with raccoons. ("Raccoons!" I said. "Don't they have rabies?") I tried not to let the information about there being a girl offstage leave me too discouraged. Wasn't I here, in the country, to get away from men just like him? Those young, drop-dead gorgeous things I saw all the time in the city, walking from an audition to a photo shoot, from a gallery opening to a sex club. Wasn't this sojourn of mine a time to repair and heal the damaged and maligned parts of me that had turned me bitter longer than this young man had been alive? I hardly imagined I would see this boyish thing again once this ride was completed. He was certain to be off to another paying customer, and I couldn't even keep a boyfriend a decade older than me interested for more than six weeks, let alone a young one who was charging me by the inch.

The cabin was exactly as Evan had described it. Down a bumpy path that was part gravel, part dirt, made from prefab wood sections, with a tiny front porch and a chimney, the whole building smaller than my Manhattan apartment. I looked at it and thought, *Oh my god, what have I gotten myself into?* Scott helped me carry my bag of books inside and when I handed him his fare, plus a too generous tip because of his youthful beauty, he handed me a business card and said, "Call us if you need anything else—to check out bear tracks. Go down to the village for supplies. Whatever."

Us, I noted him saying. Not *him*. Don't call me. Call *us*. I nodded as he left and was suddenly so worried about whether there was food in the cabin that I forgot to give him a smile and a polite good-bye. Evan had not told me if there was any food in the place, nor what I would have to do if I needed to find food. I quickly discovered some canned soup in a cabinet, but could not spot a can opener, then realized, when I turned on the faucet and the water that came out appeared brown, that I was not about to stay here in this godforsaken place unless—well, unless I could at least believe that the water was decent enough to drink.

I tried to relax for a few minutes, unpack, settle in and start a book, but my mind was consumed by the fear that there was no satisfactory drinking water. As I read, my throat became drier and drier as words raced in front of my eyes and straight out my ears. Why had I not thought this trip completely through? Why hadn't Evan told me I needed water, of all things? And food and toilet paper and a can opener if I wanted to survive? Finally, feeling as if I had been dumped in the Sahara, I went to the phone and dialed the "Us" number on the card Scott had left. When a woman finally answered (after about the six-hundredth ring), I explained my predicament and asked if someone could find me—wherever the hell in the middle of nowhere I was—and take me to a store.

By now I was sweating. It was hot outside and even hotter inside the cabin, and I felt all my body fluid flowing right through my pores. It was another ninety-minutes of sheer, dry torture before there was a knock at the door, because I was certain the woman who had taken my call was purposely trying to scare the High-Strung Undesirable I had become right back to the city where I came from. "Hey," Scott said, when I opened the door. "My mom said something happened."

I could not contain my embarrassment, felt my face redden and my throat constrict and the Mojave sand my tongue had turned into made my eyes go teary, ready to expel the last of my body's moisture. "I need to go to the store," I said rather curtly, then tried to find a way to soften my behavior, so I reached out for my crutch and hopped across the room.

"Sure," he said and started out to his truck.

He helped me shop, following me patiently through the aisles of the tiny grocery store in town. The prices were astonishingly low compared to my corner bodega in the city, though some of the items on the shelf seemed to be older than my driving-aide. Scott was a practiced companion, not wandering away, not trying to convince me to buy something I didn't want, exhibiting no signs of boredom, and my first instinct was to turn to him and ask him to marry me because he was so much more composed than any guy I had dated in the last decade and gone shopping with, but then I realized I would not be able to fight off his potentially angry, insulted youthful fists with a crutch and my unbalanced posture once he realized what I really hoped and desired of him.

His gentlemanly behavior continued even when mine did not. (I had a snippy exchange with a clerk in the meat aisle when I couldn't see where they had stamped the expiration dates on the labels.) Scott carried the bags to the truck, helped me up into the passenger seat, even carried the bags into the cabin and emptied the contents onto the counter.

When I handed him his fare and another nice tip, I asked him if he wanted to stay for something to eat. Outside, the sun was setting, though it would be another good hour before it was fully dark.

He fumbled and squirmed at my unexpected invitation and said that he'd like to but couldn't, since he had promised his mother he would be home for dinner and then there were a few things he needed to talk to his girlfriend about. *Mother. Girlfriend*—these were such strange words to me that I almost asked for a definition or explanation of the terms. I really didn't expect he would take me up on my offer, but I also didn't expect he would have one of his own. As he was walking back to his truck, his head cast down toward the ground in thought, he stopped and yelled back to ask if I liked boating.

"Boating?" I echoed back at him, not really understanding the concept of a structure floating in water—we were in a forest, of all places—I knew of no lake nearby. So I thought he might have said, *Voting. Do I like voting?*

"Yes, well, sure," I said, not wanting to displease him. I tried to sound positive and optimistic, and, well, *happy*.

Then he explained that he owned a small boat at a lake that was not far from my cabin and he needed to check up on it sometime the following day, and did I want to ride over with him to the lake—get out of the cabin for a while—and if the weather was good, we could go out for a bit on the lake.

I hung on to the *we. We could go out a bit.*

"Sure," I said, not at all worried that I was a hundred years old and had only one working leg. I closed the door dizzy and confused. Tom Sawyer had offered to take me out on his raft.

I waited and waited and waited and waited for young Tom Sawyer to show up the next morning. He called me early and said he had to run an errand for his brother, then called and said he needed to sub for his uncle for a fare in town, and then called and said he would have to drop his mother off at the church and would be over after that. It was after lunchtime when he finally showed up at the cabin, honking the truck's horn from the end of the drive.

"You ready?" he yelled out of the window, as if I had been holding him up. From the doorway I stood amazed at the impatience in his voice and I almost called out and canceled, till I noticed his smile, his too-white, beautiful nineteen-year-old smile. "Just a sec," I yelled back, then hopped to my crutch and was out the door as quick as my one old reliable leg could take me.

"It's not far," he said, when I was settled in my seat and we were headed down the small road that led to the cabin. Not far turned out to be farther than you'd think. About an hour later we reached an enormous lake where there was a small inlet in which ten boats were harbored. Scott pointed out the boat that was his, then sprang out of the truck and began unloading several bags from the back onto the dock. I hobbled over to the boat and waited for him to help me in; once he did, he began to toss the bags into the boat for me to catch. I tried to pretend that I was much stronger and more seaworthy than I really was, but each time I absorbed the weight of a bag, I felt my bum foot creak and burn with pain. Finally, when all of the bags were inside the boat, Scott began pitching them into the hold.

The boat was a small sailboat, about twenty feet in length, named *The Harbor Witch,* which I felt was an adequate description of my mood as I tried to catch my breath and keep steady. As Scott stood in the hold unloading the bags—canned foods, bottled sodas, towels, pillows, stuff like that—I stood at the doorway and watched. "It doesn't really belong to me," he said. "My brother said if I cleaned it up, I could take it out today."

At last, there it was. The catch. The glitch. It wasn't Scott's boat, it was his older brother's and he was only allowed to use it if he cleaned it up for him. "What could I possibly do?" I asked, leaning into my crutch and balancing myself as the boat wobbled in the water. I didn't expect that he would take me up on my halfhearted offer. First of all there was the crutch, which I clutched for dear life as the boat pitched back and forth. Then there was the fact that I was a guest. An invited guest. You don't ask invited guests to clean your brother's boat. Do you?

But he did. "Mop, I guess," he said.

Mop? He wants me to mop? I don't think I actually articulated my exasperation, but it must have shown in my tense, cynical, horrified urban personality and posture. Then I realized that if I stormed away in a huff I was a good hour from the cabin with no way to get back unless I called a cab. *Him.* I would have to call him.

"Or scrub if it's easier for you."

Scrub? If it's easier?

And then there was the smile. (And I suppose I should add that he was dressed in shorts and a tank top, his shoulders smooth and deeply muscled, with the silky blond hair of his armpits peeking out beneath them.) Yes, he *was* Tom Sawyer. That smile had made it impossible to resist him. He soon had me starboard on my knees washing down his brother's boat, the sun beating against the back of my neck, the cool air from the water chilling the sweat-soaked T-shirt I wore and that I refused to take off because I was too worried it would reveal the layers of fat around my waist. Scott, however, took off his tank top, and I had chance enough to stretch and look and stretch and look and stretch and look. It was a glorious thing, really, working, stopping, looking at a young god sweating underneath the summer sun.

"Don't forget to clean the grommets," he said to me.

"Uh-huh," I answered. *Of course not. Don't forget the grommets.* Wasn't there a term for this sort of role-playing I was willingly participating in? Slave and master? Sadomasochism?

We mopped and cleaned and polished and when I thought we were almost done, Scott said there was "just a little more to do." Just a little bit more turned into another thirty minutes or so, but it was such simple, honest work, cleaning, sweating and watching a beautiful young man, that I could not stop when he said we were through. In fact, I told him he had missed a spot where he had been polishing a rail and I went over and cleaned it myself.

It was late afternoon when he showed me how to rig the sails and then used the small outboard motor at the back of the boat to guide us out of the harbor. When we were far enough out in the lake, he cut the engine and the sails caught the wind. He seemed to know what he was doing, yelling at me to watch the boom, demonstrating how to tie a proper knot and guide the rudder. Of course he made me wear a life jacket, which both upset and delighted me. It showed he cared enough to worry that I might drown, but there I was, next to a shirtless sailor at the helm of a sleek vessel, inflated and bulky like a bright orange rubber duck that would not sink.

As we sailed along the lake, Scott pointed out his favorite homes on shore: the one with the best pier, another that he felt certain was big enough to turn into a nightclub. We dropped anchor in a small cove and The Young Worthy Seaman asked if I wanted to take a swim to cool off. Yes, I thought, of course I do. I need to cool off. I've had more excitement today than I've had in the last twenty years. And I wanted to swim and frolic with the Beautiful Boy of the Lake no matter how much I resembled The Ugliest and Most Awkward Pool Toy in the Store.

While Scott was in the galley doing something or other, I took off the life jacket, removed my T-shirt and shorts, unwrapped the bandage from my leg, wrapped a towel around my waist to retain my modesty (and mask my growing desire) and put the life jacket back on.

Scott helped me to the bow of the boat and we momentarily discussed the best way for me to jump into the water, whether it would hurt my leg less to fall on my good side or go straight in. He was now wearing nothing—having also shed his shorts, and I could not keep my concentration focused on how to jump when there it was, The Thing That Made Him So Young and Desirable, right there, right there beside me and in full glorious view. (And yes, he was hung, exactly as you'd expect a nineteen-year-old guy to be—a large, heavy set of balls and a pink, fleshy sausage of a cock.) Finally, I was so agitated and hot, hot, hot, that I just dropped my towel and fell overboard into the water. It was a glorious, wonderful and cooling dunk and Scott dove in as soon as he saw me bob to the surface.

Scott swam and dove beneath the water, circling the Great Orange Inflatable Head I now was, talking about this and that as he gulped for breath and tossed the water out of his hair. "This is my favorite spot," he said, and I cast my eyes around the lake and the shoreline as if we were pirates who had landed and found buried treasure. "Cindy—my girlfriend—doesn't like the boat at all. She thinks it's too much work. She'd rather have a speedboat. My brother says she just doesn't get it. Sailing. You know, all the work and lessons to feel the wind catch in the sail and carry you away. Without the motor."

I nodded and bobbed and smiled in the best way I knew. At that moment I felt happy and content; the sun was glowing orange, setting slowly in the sky; the water was warm and still around us, broken only by Scott's swimming and splashing. In the water I could move and kick my foot, whereas on land I felt useless. And for a moment I had left behind my daily urban struggles and continual boyfriend troubles. I expected nothing from Scott—certainly nothing in the romance or sex department—other than one nice surprise after another. Which was exactly what happened.

"I wish I didn't have to go back," he said. "Don't you ever wish that? That you didn't have to go back to something that you don't like when you're somewhere having a great time. Everyone's nagging me to keep applying for a job here or a job there. I just feel like I'm groveling. I want to do something I like to do and get paid for it."

"It's not easy putting yourself out there and asking for work," I said. I thought about all the jobs I had waded through in the last few years—from a publicist to a temporary office assistant to a newspaper editor to an occasional bartender until I landed in the communications office at the corporation where I had a steady position. "I'm sure you'll find a job soon. Just keep asking everyone you know. Someday, somebody will hear of something. That's usually how it works. Somebody hears of something and remembers you were looking for a job."

"But I hope I like it," he said. "That's important. I've got to want to do it. Why can't I have a job doing something like this?"

"No reason why you can't," I said. "But that means you have to really look for it. You can't wait for it to come along."

The sun was now a bright orange ball floating on the surface of the water. I imagined myself falling in love with a boy less than half my age, and it was a glorious fantasy. And for a moment I wasn't the older man. I was as young and beautiful and as eager as him. Ready to find and conquer the world.

"You know how to find the way back in the dark?" I asked.

It wasn't really an overwhelming concern, just a thought that had emerged from the back of my mind as I looked at the sun. We had stayed out later on the lake than I had expected.

"I don't have to be back till morning," he said.

That was when it struck me that we weren't rushing back so quickly. He realized his mistake immediately—of not telling me his plans for fear of my casting doubt or suspicion on them. He floundered a moment by scrunching up his face, then said, "I can take you back if you want. The boat's real comfortable though. Or we can sleep up there on the shore. I've done it before. It's real neat. Feels like you're right under the stars."

Sleep on the boat? Or outside in the wilderness? What is he thinking? Who does he think I am? Davy Crockett? I looked at the boat and then at the shore. "Okay," I said in a weakened voice. Who was I to spoil the adventure?

We decided to camp on shore. Scott got cushions from the boat and we floated various things to dry land—a blanket, towels, frying pan, canned foods, beer, matches. On shore, he spread out the blanket and I collected sticks and twigs, and we started a small fire at a spot enclosed by stones (where someone had obviously camped before).

We ate, and drank the beers and sat beneath the stars and talked. I had dressed again in my T-shirt and shorts and rewrapped my leg, but Scott sat shirtless, wearing only a towel around his waist, as if he were a native tribesman entertaining the Great Big Fat Tourist. He confessed that he'd had an argument with his girlfriend the day before; it had happened right before he picked me up at the train station and had continued throughout the day. He said she was wearing him down, pressuring him to set a date for a wedding when he knew he wasn't ready or able to commit to her yet.

"She's not the right one," he said. "But I just can't tell her that. I'm too chicken. I don't want to start her crying."

Of course, I realized exactly how the girlfriend must be feeling, loving the godlike creature he was, unable to fully snare him and make him submissive. I started thinking about all the men I had dated who were really boys at heart, emotionally distant, romantically immature, especially the ones who thought the notion of a great date with me was going to a bar and looking at *other* guys.

"How come you don't have a girlfriend?" Scott asked.

It was a quick and hypothetical question, I knew that, but my stunned silence seemed to answer part of his question, so he backtracked and amended it to, "Or a guy? A boyfriend?"

I tried not to let my memories make me feel sorry for myself. "There was someone years ago," I said. "But he died. I just haven't found anyone else who seemed right. Right for me."

"My brother says I'll know when she's right," Scott said. "He says it'll just hit me in the heart."

"Is he married?" I asked.

"Divorced," Scott said. "He said he made a big mistake marrying Melinda."

We talked about other things—favorite movies, worst TV shows, places we wanted to visit, as the dark grew deeper around us—crickets chirping, the wind rustling the leaves behind us, the fire snapping and talking as if it were another friend offering advice. We lay back on the blanket and looked at the sky and fell into a conversation about the possibility of God and our wish that He could provide us with more obvious and specific clues on how to live best.

Days later, Evan asked me why I hadn't just reached out and pounced on Scott and I tried to explain to him that it wasn't the most pressing desire of the moment, or, that, of course, it *was* the most pressing desire of the moment but that doing it, having sex—or trying to engage Scott in the possibility of sex with me—would have spoiled what was already there—a lush, romantic, sensual moment where nature displays every obvious and specific way you have been blessed.

I didn't tell Evan that I slept fitfully on the blanket, however, that I fell into one dream after another, thinking that Scott was reaching out to me, embracing me, his lips pressing mine open and his hands finding every part of me that I wanted him to find. I dreamed and dreamed and dreamed that he had moved closer, so much so that when I woke in the morning I was exhausted and hiding an erection that would not subside until the startling cold water of the lake forced it to disappear. I felt like a foggy old fool trying to keep up with Scott as we floated our things back to the boat, my throat dry, my breath stinking, what hair I still maintained spiking up in patches. Scott was unusually uneasy that next morning, as if he had made a mistake in camping out and now he was running late and he would soon be in big-time trouble with someone, and we used the motor to sail the boat back to the harbor faster.

The drive back to the cabin was quiet and respectful, but I soon began wondering if my dreams the night before had been dreams at all; maybe Scott really had reached out to me sometime during the night and was now feeling sheepish about his behavior. I tried and tried to work out if it had been a dream or real, or if it had merely been an old man's drunken memory of another lover from another time. At the cabin I invited Scott inside for breakfast or coffee or anything he wanted or needed, but he gracefully declined everything I offered and drove away, leaving me propped up on my crutches in front of the door. For the rest of the day I slept as much as I could, lifting myself back into the dream of Scott as often as possible, remembering the way he had smelled and tasted and felt in my arms—or at least as I had imagined him. After a few hours of more sleep and dreaming, I masturbated myself awake and that seemed to break the spell. I had gotten him (somewhat) out of my system and was ready to move on.

I spent the rest of my time at the cabin reading the bag of books I had brought, some worthwhile, others not so. The first day or so I hoped Scott might call again and then I thought about calling him, but I knew that it was not the right thing to do—to engage myself further in such an impossible flirtation. On my final day, I packed and called the car service to take me back to the train station. Scott's mother said someone would pick me up soon, and I sat and waited on the porch hoping it might be Scott who showed up.

It wasn't Scott who picked me up, but his uncle, a handsome man (about my age!) who clearly displayed the genetic roots of Scott's attractiveness. "You're Scottie's friend," he said, while he lifted my bag of books and heaved them into the back of the truck. "He said he had a good time out on the lake with you. Shame about your leg. Hope it's feeling better."

I nodded and smiled and we talked about the local landmarks as he drove me back toward the village and the train station.

And that was that, my one and only visit to Evan's cabin. Back in the city, it all seemed like it had happened to someone else, as if it were a scene from a movie or out of one of the books I had read.

Months later, however, when Evan was meeting his lover and some other friends at the cabin—he had been unable to leave the city at the same time as the rest of the group—he called the car service I had talked about to take him out to the cabin. He described the pickup truck exactly as I had—red and old and clunky and noisy—and mentioned that his driver was an "impossibly handsome young man." It wasn't Scott but his older brother, Ray, who was the driver, and after listening to Ray's litany of the town's landmarks—the Laundromat, the green barn, the new stone bridge—Evan asked Ray about his younger brother, explaining he had heard of Scott from a friend who had used the cabin while his leg was healing.

"He's flown the coop," Ray said, smiling and laughing as he turned onto the path that led to the cabin. "He got his sorry ass out of here as soon as he wised up to that girl who was chasing him. He never really wanted to stay, you know? He's got the family wild streak bad. He's working down in Florida now, taking tourists out on fishing boats or out sailing. He's out doin' the world. Seein' what he can see."

"I'm glad he went for the adventure," I told Evan when he relayed the story to me later, sometime after my leg had healed and I was once again hunting for a new boyfriend. "Sounds like he's happy—doing what he should be doing."

TRUE IN MY FASHION

Paul Brownsey

I am very happy with Kenneth, but the relationship involves a lie. I told it thirty-three years ago.

If you distinguish big lies from little lies, mine was only a little lie. It isn't, for instance, that I have a wife and children but have lied to keep them from Kenneth's knowledge all these years.

Nor is my lie anything like that told to me by someone I was with before Kenneth, a person who said he was a television producer for BBC Scotland. I thought his rundown, two-room flat in Partick was a bit of a dump for a top BBC producer, but he said it was just a pied-à-terre and that his real home was a big house in Helensburgh where, unfortunately, we couldn't go because his mother lived there. One room had bare boards and an old vinyl settee and a TV. The other contained a cooker and dripping sink, a wee Formica-topped table, three stacking chairs, a shower cabinet, and a mattress on the floor where we had sex.

Once, he told me that Debbie Harry was coming to dinner with us at the pied-à-terre. Then the story was that she'd cancelled because of flying to New York to record a duet with Darryl Hall but had sent me a present as an apology. I looked at the album, which was signed in her name with love to me, and thought how the bedsheets always reeked of cooking smells, which implied he stayed there a lot.

One night, Kenneth came up to me in the bar and told me that my BBC producer was just a clerk in Glasgow Council's cleansing department.

When I learned he wasn't what he'd said he was, I wasn't upset or angry with him. You need to know a person for that, and here I felt I did not know anyone, because he'd deceived me about himself. If a tree in the park dematerialized before my eyes, I wouldn't feel shock or alarm, because it would be too weird and disorienting for ordinary feelings.

No, my lie was nothing gross like that.

My lie was to claim to have written a poem I hadn't. In fact, the poem was a song lyric by Irving Berlin.

Kenneth was chunky and open faced and bright eyed. He said "great stuff" and "okeydokey" a lot, and he soon adopted "no problemo" when it came in. At first I treated all this as a front behind which there had to be weakness and self-doubt, but by the time he spilled the beans about my TV producer/cleansing clerk, I'd never noticed a single chink in him through which that stuff could be glimpsed. It still amazes me that in those days Kenneth could be so ready to live together, buy a house together and so on, without any fear of going public as a gay couple, exposed to neighbors and family and employers, whereas this fear pervaded most of us so completely we didn't realize it was there and thought we were caused to act only by passion or its absence.

He said he was telling me about the TV producer/housing clerk because he wanted to protect me from hurt and then I heard coming from the dance floor Debbie Harry singing "Heart Of Glass." It was hard not to see this as a sign, a record by someone about whom I'd been lied to playing just when I'd been enlightened about the man who told the lie and forged Debbie Harry's signature and love on the album.

Actually, I knew there were no signs and everything was just chance.

I said to Kenneth, "May I have this dance with you?" Note the phrase.

Later that night, in bed, he said to me, "You were so formal," and he laughed. It wasn't the hurtful mocking laughter of someone who sits outside the world and finds you an object of amusement, but the upholding laughter that spills over from love.

He said, laughing again, "So formal that I was expecting you to say, 'May I perform fellatio upon you?'" Then he hugged me like he was a wall against the world, and so we were happy together at once.

Be patient. I am getting to my lie.

I love musicals, though now I have to keep the fact from Kenneth. I once read that Irving Berlin wrote a huge number of songs in which some aspect of dancing features as a metaphor for some aspect of love: "Change Partners" and "Cheek To Cheek" and "Let's Face The Music And Dance" and "It Only Happens When I Dance With You," et cetera. One of his early efforts was "May I Have This Life With You?" This, obviously, is a play upon the traditional formal request for a dance—the formal request that Kenneth laughed at in such a wonderful way the night we became an item. Berlin wrote it to the tune that he later recycled as "The Hostess With The Mostest" in *Call Me Madam*. Berlin did that sort of thing. The song everyone knows as "Easter Parade" began life as "Smile And Show Your Dimple."

Well, because "May I Have This Life With You?" echoed what I had said to Kenneth on our first night and also because the words expressed what I truly felt and still feel, I wrote the lyric in my first Valentine to him:

May I have this life with you-oo?
Let me take you by the hand.
It's a life just made for two-oo,
Dancing to a ragtime band.
And if we match steps to the rhythm this whole life through
We'll be in each other's arms for the next one too.

"Did you write this?" he asked. Of course he got the allusion to my invitation at once. He gave his laugh that honors a treasured possession.

"Yes."

I'm not going to deny responsibility and say, *I don't know what came over me,* or *It was just a sudden mad impulse.* In olden days people might even have said, *An evil spirit spoke through me.* Being that I'm a human not possessed by a demon, lies don't just pop out of me. And it would be dishonest to pretend that my *yes* referred only to the physical act of writing the lyric on the card.

After I said, "Yes," Kenneth kissed me and said, "Re your request re having this life with me, no problem at all."

I hear you saying, *Is that it?* That's *your lie? Come on! It was harmless enough.*

Or: *Well, if you are so troubled by it decades later, just tell him.*

No.

Would he dump you for having lured him in by deceit and false pretenses?

Of course not. Our love has acquired its own weight and permanence totally independent of that lie.

Well, there you are, then. Tell him, and he'll laugh—you go on about his laughter. You'll laugh together, *the moment will enhance you both, and then you can move on.*

I cannot tell him. I don't tell lies. That is who I am. I'm not like my BBC producer/cleansing clerk.

My lie has had consequences.

I was afraid that Kenneth might find me out. He delights so much in pleasing me that it would have been like him to seek out recordings of little-known musicals as gifts. I pictured something arriving from America with a title like *The Unknown Irving Berlin*. Removing it from its packaging prior to wrapping it in beautiful gift wrap for my birthday or Christmas he glances at the list of the titles, and, since he can never forget the words of my first Valentine to him, it leaps out at him: "May I Have This Life With You?" Out of curiosity he plays it. He discovers I lied.

So I made a point of saying from time to time, "I don't know why, but I've gone off musicals, somehow." When he got us tickets for the 1987 London production of *Follies*, I gave a complicated performance in which I acted the delight I really felt but deliberately added apparently unintentional hints that I was only pretending to be pleased so as to not to hurt his feelings. ("I don't know why, but I've gone off musicals, somehow, but, of course, *this* is different.") The more successful I was in this, the more I hurt his feelings, but needs must.

The consequences did not stop there. Although I *said,* "I don't know why, but I've gone off musicals, somehow," I hadn't, and when the CD era hit its stride and there was a vogue for reissuing old musicals on CD, I couldn't resist. Such treasures! Of course, things like the original Broadway cast album of *My Fair Lady* and the soundtracks of the main Rodgers and Hammerstein films would always be available, reissued again and again. But there was a lot of stuff that would only have a brief life in the catalogues, long-forgotten Broadway musicals like *Christine*, starring Maureen O'Hara, no less. So I bought them but hid them. I told Kenneth that one drawer contained all my childhood diaries and while, of course, he could read them if he wanted to—for there were no secrets between us—still, I said, I had a sort of irrational squeamishness about anyone reading them. Which of course produced a promise he wouldn't look at them.

"Anyway," he said, "they wouldn't show me the you that I love. Love this whole life through, remember?"

You may be thinking that this is a moralistic lesson about how one lie leads to more lies, a web of lies, like in "For Want of a Nail..." the kingdom was lost.

No, that's not the point at all.

But when, you might say, *did you listen to these CDs? Surely it was no different from not having them at all, not being able to play them?*

Oh, but possession is a bulwark.

And something might happen that would allow me to play them freely, for instance, Kenneth's death.

Of course, they might undergo that process of CD decay called bronzing and become unplayable, but to be on the safe side I stored second copies of particular favorites, preferably different pressings so that if one bronzed the other might not. I also started secretly putting them on an MP3 player, but Kenneth isn't often away so I don't get much opportunity for that.

Sometimes I take a horrifying risk. I put a show musical CD in a classical music case and in Kenneth's presence put on the CD and listen to it through headphones. Suppose Kenneth suddenly notices the CD case while I am listening to, say, *Kiss Me, Kate*, and says, "Hey, Beethoven's Fifth, fantastico," and presses the button to channel the sound through the loudspeakers? That would crack open all the defenses that the world has put in place.

There's safer listening to my show music CDs when Kenneth's dad calls saying he's scared he might have a stroke and lie there unfound. Then Kenneth goes and spends a night or two at his sheltered housing—he won't come here because he's homophobic—and while Kenneth sleeps badly on the settee and cleans the house and helps the old man shuffle to and from the bathroom, I enjoy the guilty pleasure of *Belle*, a 1961 British musical about wife-murderer Dr. Crippen that flopped in the West End, or *Skyscraper*, a dull and awkward Broadway musical from 1965 starring Julie Harris that's redeemed by one song, the sublime, "I'll Only Miss Her When I Think Of Her," which, when I play it, in my mind changing the sex like in the Peggy Lee recording, is about me thinking of Kenneth at his dad's.

Sometimes on these evenings alone I think it would be only poetic justice if it were I, not Kenneth's dad, who had the stroke and died alone. Kenneth would find me stretched out cold, the musicals CDs lying around the living room to prove my untruthfulness, while blasting again and again on repeat, Mitzi Gaynor sings about being, like I am, in love with a wonderful guy.

But if this poetic justice occurred, it would have this comfort: there is a pattern, the universe is being administered, things happen because they are meant to, the risk is not from chance events.

Of course, someday I shall indeed die, and Kenneth, sorting my things, will unlock the drawer. If he was telling the truth when he said he didn't want to read my diaries, he won't discover it's locked till then. He'll then discover I lied about its containing diaries and lied about having gone off musicals, but discovering these lies won't reveal my lie about the poem. Still, it will be like the stashes of pornography that wives sometimes find and write to agony aunts about: *To think that when we make love he is fantasizing about...suddenly a stranger to me...never known him at all.* And he won't be able to tell himself they're just a hangover from the days when I liked musicals, because a lot of them have recent issue dates on them. I don't like to leave Kenneth with all that distress, but there is something in me, some little core of self-destruction or self-preservation, that prevents my getting rid of my show music CDs, and I wouldn't do it even if I managed to put them all on my MP3 player.

But I'm not without a way forward.

I have evidence that would allow me to believe that Kenneth has forgotten that I wrote what I did in that card. In itself that's sad, but the good outweighs the evil. Safety is part of the quality of life, not a substitute for it.

There's a program about musicals on the radio on Sunday afternoons, usually hosted by Elaine Paige.

One Sunday the program came on unexpectedly while I was making dumplings in the kitchen, dough all over my fingers. It would have been too significant, too likely to arouse suspicion of a weakness in my defenses, to go across and turn it off with mucky fingers. Kenneth was cleaning his shoes and mine at the back door behind me.

Elaine started talking about composers recycling things. Richard Rodgers recycled "Beneath The Southern Cross" from *Victory At Sea* as "No Other Love" in *Me And Juliet.* "Getting To Know You" in *The King And I* began life as "Suddenly Lovely" for *South Pacific.*

Furiously, I scraped surplus dough off my fingers with the kitchen knife.

"Say A Prayer For Me Tonight," cut from *My Fair Lady*, ended up in *Gigi*. "And," said Elaine, "Irving Berlin's 'Hostess With The Mostest'—"

The scraped-off dough was bloody, a little flap of skin hung from a finger.

"—started life like *this!*"

And the opening lines of "May I Have This Life With You?" began, sung by an ancient crackly male voice.

May I have this life with you-oo?

Let me take you by the hand...

The gushing of the cold water on my finger wasn't enough to drown out the ancient crackly male voice.

Shouting and hollering about my wound would create a diversion but something stopped me.

...It's a life just made for two-oo...

Now Kenneth was actually singing along, shoe-brushing to the rhythm.

And then Ethel Merman's abrasive voice poured out relief upon me as the engineers did a clever thing, seamlessly merging "May I Have This Life With You?" into "The Hostess With The Mostest." A comet out of nowhere had missed the earth by a hairsbreadth and was now on its way back to outer space.

I mean, he knew the words but he didn't say he'd recognized them as what I'd written in my card, did he? So I don't have to think he did.

"You know," Kenneth said, gathering up the shoe-cleaning stuff, "I don't know why, but I could quite get to like musicals, somehow. Christ, what have you done?"

I don't know why, but I've gone off musicals, somehow. Yes, what he said echoed what I'd said, but so what? It's well known that couples unconsciously influence each other.

"Give me your hand," he said. "Let me take you by the hand. May I perform first aid upon you?" he said, dabbing and pressing my bloody finger with sheets of kitchen towel until the blood stopped flowing. He fetched and attached a plaster. It was grubbied by a fingerprint of shoe polish because he'd been too caught up in alarm about me to wash his hands first.

"All mended," he said.

"Well..."

"No problemo. No problem at all."

So the chance event of this radio program has opened the way to a scenario that saves the situation. I can choose in all honesty to believe that Kenneth has forgotten I quoted the lyric in my card; meanwhile, he gets to really like musicals, which allows me to discover that actually I like them after all (*I don't know why, but I've gone onto musicals again, somehow*), which means we start buying lots of show music CDs (*It's much nicer to have the physical object than just to download them*), which allows me gradually to slip in among the ones on our open shelves the ones from the locked drawer, which means I prevent the shameful revelation after I am dead that I lied about going off musicals, which lie was to prevent him discovering the lie about the lyric I told thirty-three years ago. The world survives, renews itself, and Kenneth's love continues to protect me from bad things breaking in, although, of course, because of his love nothing was ever really at risk anyway.

SIGHT

Jordan Taylor

Archer's voice mingled with rushing waves and biting wind as he spoke into my ear. "There's a ship. State ferry, car and passenger, white and green. Seagulls catching rides in the wake."

Sunlight soaked my left side. Archer stood against my right. A mix of musty, salty odors swirled through the breeze amidst a cacophony of waves. Dead crabs, live fish, decomposing seaweed, rotting driftwood, all churned through ocean brine that haunted the nose like a brilliant flash haunts the eyes. And wet dog. Luath leaned against my left leg. Even off duty, I carried her harness and she would hardly leave my side.

"Can you get Luath to chase the birds? She's not having much fun."

"She won't listen to me."

"You tease her."

"The gulls moved on." A pause as Archer's head turned beside mine. "Crows on driftwood up the beach behind us. Luath, *look*, go get the birds."

I felt him fling out his arm to point for her.

Luath didn't move, her warm presence shielding my legs from wind.

"Sometimes I think she doesn't trust me," Archer said, his lips brushing my ear.

Wasn't he self-conscious on the public beach, his arm across my waist? He used to be stressed about those things. I could hear only waves, wind, a few birds, Luath panting by my knee, though I knew we stood not far from campsites.

"I don't blame her," I said.

"No? You trust her more than me?"

"I've learned from experience to second guess your directions more than hers. Human errand. Nothing personal."

Another pause; only wind twisted past. Then Archer said, "You mean, 'human error'?"

"That's what I said."

"You said 'errand.'"

"Close enough."

"What dictionary are you using?"

Luath nudged the harness in my hand. I didn't like this part; making judgments to say if your dog was better off doing the work she loved, or imposing freedom. At least she had managed some relaxation over the past few days in the San Juans.

"No criticizing on vacation," I said, opening buckles on the harness.

"Don't you mean, 'No cannibalizing on vacation'? That would be close enough."

"God, Archer, you're worse than my mother. It's not a crime to get a word wrong."

"Maybe not, if you haven't swallowed a library."

I bent to harness Luath. She licked my hands, wagging her whole rear against my legs.

Archer chuckled. “Such a blonde.”

“Now you’re cannibalizing my dog.”

“Did you really just say that?”

I stood up with the harness handle and short, leather leash to her collar in my left hand.

“I’m not criticizing your dog.” I heard the grin in his voice as he put his arm around me once more, leaning into my right shoulder, kissing my ear. “I love your dog. I love you, Noah.”

“Overcompensating.”

“Sorry.”

“Isn’t the sun setting? Should we start for camp?”

“Camp?” His lips curved upward against my neck. “You mean the eight-bedroom, turreted, hillside Victorian B and B we’re staying in?”

“Shall we go?”

“It’s just before the show starts. The sky’s blinding, golden white, then bright blue.”

A car engine sounded far off. Campers packing on Sunday evening after a weekend of Pacific Northwest sand and sun. Perhaps we were within sight of other tourists after all, yet Archer remained against me, talking into my ear about colors, waves, seabirds.

I dropped the harness handle to reach for Luath’s silky head, resting my fingers across the curve of her skull.

“It’s sinking,” Archer said.

Good. Nearly time to go. For our last night here maybe Archer would humor me with carryout pizza or fish and chips so we didn’t have to eat in public.

“Yellow, turning orange, turning pink,” Archer said. “There’s another ship. Looks like it’s plated in gold. The seagulls’ wings are flashing flames, slicing through the sky. Every wave catches the light as it turns and falls, like a dance with a million performers.”

"How about the sand?" I asked.

"Where it's wet from receding tide, it catches light like glass. Like it's been melted down in a forge."

He kissed me again, letting his lips linger on my skin so I felt his nose, chin, eyelashes, the warmth of his breath on my neck. And sudden tension in his body.

I started to turn my head. "Archer?"

"Noah, will you marry me?"

Wind stopped roaring. Waves stopped crashing. Luath stopped panting. I felt her turn, shift in the harness to look up while my muscles grew rigid as driftwood, holding my breath. Smells vanished with sounds. Void. Empty. Nothing.

"*No.*" I snapped the word, not like a refusal, but an order, a challenge, even a threat. I snatched Luath's harness handle and wheeled away while my words to her were barely formed. "Luath, *left. Forward.*"

We made an about turn, started up the beach toward the hillside Victorian a quarter of a mile away. Luath rushed across wet sand, pulling me with her faster than I would normally allow. As if we could outrun the question, leave it buried in the sand, never to be heard from again.

I met Archer in our freshman year of high school, after his family moved to Olympia in February. When not in class, he spent much of his time until summer break standing in any uninhabited nook of the grounds. No reading, talking, texting. He stood, waiting for the bell to ring, nearly invisible.

To my later regret, I couldn't remember details of the first moment I saw him. I did remember the first time I *looked* at him.

Archer stood in the rain, one sneaker in beauty bark around a raised flowerbed, the other foot propped on the brick edge of the bed. His black hoodie drooped across his shoulders with the weight of rain, blue jeans turned navy by water, sticking to his legs like plastic wrap. He gazed at the ground, chin tipped down. Brown hair fell across his forehead, flattened, darkened and spiky from rain running through it, across his head, over his face, dripping off his pointed nose and chin in ribbons of icy water.

I had never been in love, though I had a crush on a teacher in junior high and would have given my left arm to be Peter Parker's sidekick—comic, movie, anywhere. So I wasn't sure how I knew I'd fallen in love in five seconds. But I did.

That night, I started a new comic while my parents went through their customary after-dinner shouting match downstairs and Shiloh danced in her room, listening to Kelly Clarkson. Though Shiloh was five years younger than me, I let her work on my comics. She had a genius for plot twists that went far beyond her years. I drew while she announced ideas.

This time I closed my door, starting a new notebook of sketches that no one in my family would be allowed to see.

I can still envision that first sketch: the gray, dull light; water sliding through his hair, down his temples; perfect shape of his nose and chin; curve and angle of his body against muted school grounds; low brick wall of the dead, dirt flowerbed; fixed stare into nothing.

I approached Archer the next day. Confidence, like art, was a family trait. I'd hawked my mom's handmade jewelry and paintings at art fairs for as long as I could remember, argued with my sister about the colors she chose to match—pink and orange were favorites—since she was old enough to dress herself, and learned to sneer at "imitators" by the age of ten.

"Hey," I said to Archer through the crowd as he closed his locker. "Want to hang out sometime? Do you play MMOGs?"

He stared at me, hostile blue eyes sunken against dark circles. For the first time it occurred to me that he looked like someone who hadn't had a proper night's sleep—or meal—in weeks. He seemed about to curl his lip. Instead, he walked away. Not a word.

Mouth open, I stood in the hallway like a moron while students flowed past. Perhaps he hadn't heard properly in the commotion of the hall.

Next time I tried, later that day after lunch, I abandoned the smile. "What's your problem? Got some invisible friends here already?"

He turned from dropping a sandwich bag in the trash and directed a cold stare at me. "Leave me alone."

Archer was an expert at cold stares, brows drawn close over blue eyes. I couldn't get my breath, hands clenched into fists just to resist reaching for him, room whirling like a massive top.

His expression changed. "You all right?"

I still couldn't breathe properly. "I'm—ssss—"

"What?"

"Sorry to bother you."

He turned away.

"Wait!" Several people still eating looked around. "I didn't mean sorry and we're done. I meant sorry and could we start over?"

"With what?" Though he glanced at me, he spoke through set teeth, as if he didn't want anyone to notice he was talking to me.

"I can't remember your name."

He stood there.

"Could you tell me?"

"Archer."

"That's a cool name."

Nothing.

"I'm Noah."

He looked at the clock on the wall over the cafeteria doors.

"Do you like comic books?"

"No."

"Movies?"

"No."

"You don't like movies?"

He shrugged. "I've got to go."

"The bell hasn't rung. Computers?"

He glanced at me.

"We've got a new one—old one expired—and the new one's a bitch. Can't figure out half the software on it. My mom can't stand it. I'm hoping for my own laptop for my birthday, but this is what we've got now."

He looked at me.

The bell rang.

"Can you come over after school? My mom picks me up. Stay for dinner and you can tell me how to work the desktop? If you're there, my parents won't shout at each other. We act like normal people when we have company."

It turned out Archer knew more about computers than Mom did about van Gogh—whose Wikipedia article she was always tweaking. He could take them apart, put them together, tell what everything did. He also programmed.

Our friendship developed along with the game we made—me drawing animation, Archer programming characters to run, jump, shoot crossbows. Mom adored him—such a polite, quiet young man. Shiloh could hardly be in the same room with him without being red faced and tongue-tied.

I never had to come out to my family. Which seemed lucky, though there was something to be said for an exchange of feelings. My father had appeared resigned from the day he tried to take me fishing. I vomited in the boat at the sight of his impaling a living worm on a silver hook. Then screamed like a toddler when he got me to grab a thrashing fish he swung aboard. I was thirteen. He invited Shiloh after that. Shiloh loved murdering fish, then frying them herself, eating hot, greasy flesh with her fingers like a barbarian. He never mentioned taking me again.

My mother was slightly more direct, telling me, shortly after I started bringing Archer home, that she one-hundred-percent supported whoever I wished to be with as long as that person was positive for me. And had good taste.

Archer was far better for me than I realized. I wasn't sure if he'd always been a brooding introvert, but he'd been handed an extra helping of brooding before he moved to Olympia. His father, a cop, was killed working a nightshift the previous summer. Archer and his mother moved from Saint Paul to live with his grandparents until they could "get things worked out." It would be two years before Archer said more to me about his father beyond the fact that he was dead.

In the fall of our junior year, we sat at the computer for a typical programming session while Mom was out fetching Thai food and Shiloh talked on the phone upstairs. Archer typed, checking multiple screens, programming the game, sitting up straight in the desk chair as he worked on a high-jump for a humanoid cat character. I sat on a kitchen stool behind him, resting my chin on his shoulder. We had yet to progress beyond kisses. Archer, who viewed sitting near each other in a theater or school auditorium as tantamount to a public make-out session, made it clear things were already moving plenty fast.

I blew gently in his ear to get a rise out of him.

He opened the game screen and pointed. "That what you wanted?"

"It's perfect."

"You didn't even look."

I leaned forward, my chest against his shoulder. Something

blocked the screen, like mud around the edges. I blinked, rubbed my eyes, looked again. The screen appeared normal. The catman sprang onto a platform like our human hero never could have.

"Something wrong?"

"Nothing. It's incredulous."

"What? You mean 'incredible'?"

"Awesome, perfect, rhetorical."

"Rhetorical?" He shook his head, trying not to laugh. "What was that meant to be?"

"You did a great job. Thank you." I kissed his neck.

He jumped away: Mom was unlocking the front door.

If I'd been asked, I couldn't have said what went wrong looking at the screen.

When visual glitches persisted, I kept them to myself. My parents inched closer to divorce every month. At the same time, I was in the process of getting my license. If I sometimes couldn't see my sketchbook or classroom perfectly, it wasn't a big deal compared to driving and divorce.

I might have gone longer in silence if not for the driving. I picked Shiloh up from school one day when our mom couldn't make it. A few blocks from the crowded lot, Shiloh screamed.

"Noah! What's your problem?"

"Don't shout at me when I'm driving!"

"Don't run freaking stop signs then!"

I glanced in the side mirror. My hands shook on the wheel and I took a slow breath.

"We could've been hit," she snapped. "Or arrested."

"I'm sorry. I'm really sorry. I didn't see it."

"It's a huge red sign, Noah."

Of course, Shiloh spilled the beans. I admitted to my mom that I'd had visual problems lately, though they hadn't seemed like such a big deal.

Driving privileges were suspended.

The next day, I stood in the optometrist's office, staring at everything. Drinking in the light through blinds making bars across the table of magazines, glossy and neatly arranged in rows. Water tank with tiny paper cups. Kids' toys, red, yellow, blue, wood and plastic; an old, battered Etch A Sketch.

There had never been so much to see. It was as if I'd grown up living inside a grocery store and only ever tried white bread and milk. Every art museum my mom ever dragged us to as kids, every school trip, every sketch and comic and movie. Every glance out the window. How could it be possible that I'd never really *thought* about sight?

I imagined they wouldn't know. They'd send me for tests, decide treatment. Worst case, they'd cut open my eyes with lasers and I'd have recovery time ahead and photophobia.

But the doctor did know: worse, much worse than anything we could have imagined.

Retinitis pigmentosa. A fancy name for a disease that eats the eyes. Incurable. Possibly leading to permanent and complete blindness within a year, or five, or ten.

At home, bewildered, shocked, with my equally lost and shocked mother, I went to bed and stared at my sketch of Archer in the rain. And stared. As if I would never get another chance.

Far from never seeing him again, Archer got me through the next years. My family was also there, more or less. But I never mentioned a lot of things to them. I never told them that by the time I was seventeen—seeing the world as dots in the center of my remaining field of vision—I'd made up my mind to kill myself. I told only Archer.

"You coward," he growled, sitting on my bed one Saturday afternoon. "Do you have any idea how many tens of thousands of blind people are living and working and thriving in the world right now? Grow some, Noah. God."

I sat on the edge of the bed beside him. "You don't know what it's like."

"I know what it's like when someone you love is dead." He spoke so fiercely, I leaned away. "What it feels like when you would kill to have him back, trade your life to bring him back. And you can't. There's *nothing* you can do.

"You'll excuse me for thinking you can buck up and work hard and go on living a productive life. At least no one shot you six times in the face and left you on a street corner in the middle of the night."

We sat in silence until Shiloh shouted upstairs, asking if we wanted to call for pizza.

When we stood, I finally muttered, "I won't kill myself."

"Thanks," Archer said, walking out. Leaving me to make my own way downstairs.

Other days, Archer lay on the floor with me, letting me run my fingertips over his lips, cheeks, jaw, eyebrows, eyelids, through his hair, across his ear, down his neck and shoulder. I turned my head, shifting my eyes to see fragments of him, memorize the blue eyes so adept at frigid disdain. His sharp profile. His expression, not of pity or grief or the anger flooding my own family, but of determination and concentration.

I wasn't completely blind until I was eighteen. Two years to brood, run from it, before it settled. Right about the time the divorce was finalized, Shiloh started high school, and we moved into a smaller house. I hated that new house. Shiloh went over it with me again and again. I yelled at her when she wasn't fast enough to keep me from kicking a coffee table or knocking against a doorway because I pulled too far to the right of her guiding arm.

"Can't you watch where you're going and warn me?"

"What the hell do you think I'm trying to do?"

She stopped offering to show me around after that.

I learned Braille, took up listening to audio books with the frequency of an addict and finished high school a year late.

Archer started college in Seattle, interning at the same time, helping program the next generation of smartphones or tablets or antivirus software. I told him to move on, find a normal boyfriend, at which he only sighed.

Shiloh had me pursuing a guide dog by then. With the waiting list so long and me so young and new at this, I had low expectations. I rarely left home except for eye exams or other blindness-related appointments.

It took a year before my mom put her foot down and said I was acting like a child. She drove me to an agency we'd visited early on that specialized in assisting people in my situation They were able to place me in a job. Unfortunately, it was telemarketing for a group of tree-huggers. It thrilled my mom and secured me a place in her house.

The people at the agency were adamant that nothing was impossible and I should continue my education. Blind people were teachers, musicians, writers, accountants, psychologists and lawyers. No reason to stay on a phone forever. No limits, they said. Full, productive life.

When not making phone calls about greenhouse gas or airborne particulate matter, or using my audio email interface, I did sit-ups as I listened to books, wishing Archer wasn't so painfully far away, though I told myself he needed to stay as far from me as possible.

My mom's house was a two-story shack at the edge of a block of condominiums from the 1970s. A tiny park bordered the backyard beyond a dilapidated fence. On weekends when he visited, Archer and I walked the park, or sat on a bench in the sun, saying practically nothing. No touching in public or private. I wondered if he had anyone else. I never asked.

With school out for the summer, though he was still working, Archer came around more. He told me what he saw as we walked. He never used generalities as Shiloh did: "There's a tree. Don't hit it." He used specifics: "There's a Madroño just to your right. Red bark strips are peeling back in little rows like parchment curled into scrolls. The trunk underneath is soft green, smooth and clean looking. There's a trail of ants scurrying up and down it."

Later, I started prompting for certain things: What color were the little league uniforms at the park's diamond? Was the groundskeeper using a push mower or a riding one? What kind of bird? What kind of trees?

The summer we both turned twenty, Archer rented a studio off campus and invited me over. New place. I refused, asked him over instead.

I asked how his mother was ("Depressed.") and his grandparents ("Glad I'm doing something productive.") while we shared pizza on the couch. It was like being sixteen again, no one else home, talking over our plans for the games we created.

My face felt stiff and uncomfortable. I wiped my fingers on a paper towel, reached up, discovered I was smiling.

"What's wrong?" Archer asked, close beside me.

I shook my head.

He cleared our plates. I listened as he washed his hands in the kitchen and asked if I wanted something to drink. I heard footsteps, soft on carpet in the family room, then his flopping back beside me.

"Don't you ever think of moving out?" He ran his fingers across the back of my neck, up through my hair.

I leaned away. "Of course. Just not much of a self-starter these days."

"Want to stay with me for a while? You could find a lot of new opportunities in the city."

"Olympia's a city." I turned my head, frowning at his voice.

He kissed me.

I pushed him away. "Stop it. Don't you meet people in school? I told you to find someone else."

"When have I ever listened to you?"

I opened my mouth, closed it, bit my lip. "That's not—"

"You could try it. I'm not about to add you to my lease. Just try something new."

"You don't have time to be a babysitter," I muttered.

"I don't intend to be."

"I have to get to appointments, and I'd be looking for another job—"

"Call a cab, get a bus, walk. You're not helpless. I'll show you around the neighborhood." He kissed me again.

I didn't push him away.

The studio turned out to be easy to navigate. His neighborhood had audio crosswalks and I'd gotten good enough with my collapsible white cane that I could get around within a few blocks of the place.

I found a customer service job with a local company growing enough that they needed business hours phone support. Imagining I would hate it, I found few people were really nasty on the phone and most seemed grateful when I could get them the information they needed. A tiny thing, yet it felt good to be the one doing something for someone else.

We moved into a ground-floor condo near campus. It had two bedrooms and stairs that had to be counted and mastered. Archer was back in school. I worked, hoping to return to school and get off the phone.

Archer became a hero with my family. Shiloh still had a borderline crush on him. Mom treated him like the second coming. Or maybe she treated him like he'd saved her son's life.

My dad called now and then, took me to dinner one Saturday, then asked me to his place in Olympia every other month or so after he saw eating out was not my favorite. We never had much to say to each other, mostly talking about work and jobs. I hoped that, like my mom and sister, he was glad Archer motivated me out of the house and into a more independent future. I had to hope because we never mentioned Archer.

The year that both of us turned twenty-two, with Archer just out of school and focused on a programming career, the news came about the dog. Archer took time off, begged his grandparents for a loan, and the two of us flew to Sacramento for the training period.

I wanted a German shepherd dog. I'd imagined myself walking the streets, proud and upright with a big, strong, male German shepherd in harness since Shiloh first brought up the idea.

But recipients didn't choose their dogs, and I learned that German shepherds were not popular as service dogs. The wagging, licking animal introduced to me was a silky angel. Soft, smooth, smelling of lavender and dog breath, pressing her nose against my neck as I slid from my chair to the floor.

They taught us to work together over the next weeks living at the facility. Of course, Luath already knew everything. I was the one who needed training. Archer came and went a couple of times. Then they all arrived unannounced for graduation. Even my dad.

I hugged him, trying hard not to cry as he whispered, "I'm proud of you, Noah."

Luath changed everything. Not just with my mobility. She changed who I was, how people saw me and interacted with me. She opened doors in so much more than a literal sense. People stopped to speak to me, offered help in the street, asked her name, her age, said how beautiful she was.

"Such a gorgeous dog. She's almost white."

"My cousin breeds white golden retrievers. Do you mind if I take a picture?"

"I'll bet that dog's smarter than most people. And never complains about a day's work."

Luath lived for work. And for me. I found I had much more to live for than I'd imagined after that day I ran a stop sign when I was sixteen. Since then, I'd finished fifteen hundred classic and modern books, nearly all in audio, three or four in Braille. I'd consumed a library and wanted to teach literature. I didn't know exactly how to get from where I was to where I wanted to be, but I knew a bachelor's in education was a beginning. I applied to start college in the fall.

One morning in April, I heard Luath barking with irritation as Archer teased her by bouncing her ball against the wall.

"You two are just alike," he said.

I heard her run out with the ball and knew she'd hide it in her bed.

"You're the common demeanor," I said.

"*Denominator.*" Archer shifted, sighed. I knew he had his hands on his hips.

"Don't stare at me in that tone. You're the one causing trouble."

"What, pray tell, is the tone of my stare?"

"Patronizing, disbelieving, annoyed."

Luath's claws clicked on hardwood as she trotted into the

room to rest her head on my knee. I sat at the kitchen table in front of my morning coffee.

"Want to go jogging with us this morning?" Archer asked.

"Are you talking to me or her? Breakfast?"

"Sure. What are you fixing?"

"I thought you might fix something."

Archer chuckled and walked away. Luath ran after him to hover over her bed, making sure he didn't get any ideas.

I had scrambled eggs and toast ready when he returned. I listened to his running shoes on wood. He stepped up beside me, arms around me, chin on my shoulder.

"Orange juice? Want to go away for a long weekend?"

"How?"

"I'll get a day off. They won't fire me. I was thinking the San Juans. After spring break, before summer break, sun and minimal traffic." After a pause, he added, "On me."

"Sounds great." I turned my head to kiss him.

Luath loved the big Victorian—painted pink and white outside and in, according to Archer. She nosed into every corner of our room, groveling before the resident cat while off duty.

On Saturday night, Archer took me for dinner at a quiet place with murmuring couples and a warm spot from the middle of the table where a candle burned. Much as I hated eating out, Luath, more than Archer, had taught me I wasn't the only person in the relationship.

Then on Sunday he stood against me at sunset, telling me about molten sand and dancing water, and asked me to marry him.

Back home, I wouldn't talk about it. When Archer left for work, I packed a duffel for me, another for Luath's food, toys and brushes, and then called a cab. I rode all the way to Olympia with Luath across my lap.

No one was home. I found the hidden key under the broken brick on the window ledge and let myself in. Luath knew the place. I removed her harness, gave her water in the kitchen, sat on the couch until my sister got home.

About to graduate high school, Shiloh was tall, outgoing, and had half the males in school chasing her. She still loved art and breakup songs.

"Hello stranger." She dropped her bag on the old chair with a great banging and creaking. "What are you two doing here?" She patted Luath while Luath danced about her, claws hushed on old carpet.

"Just needed a break."

"A break? You're not here for the dazzling company? What happened?"

I shrugged. "Do you have anything to eat here? I kind of missed breakfast. And lunch."

She plunked down on the couch beside me, Luath leaping up between us. "What happened, Noah? I thought you were on a trip with Archer."

"Got back yesterday."

"And?"

I shrugged again.

"Stop it."

"I just thought I'd stay awhile. If Mom doesn't mind. And if there's any food."

"You want a sandwich? I was thinking about turkey on rye."

"Sure, thanks."

She stood. "Mom's going to want to know what happened."

Of course, I wasn't able to ignore their questions. During dinner of vegetable stir fry on rice, I halted the conversation with, "Archer asked me to marry him. So I left."

The room went silent. No-breath silent. Then they continued eating without a word.

I returned to my old room and ignored Archer's calls. My mother and sister went about their business. I worked from home, listened to books, and went out with Luath because she needed the exercise, not because I wanted to go anywhere.

After three nights, Archer showed up on a workday morning. I opened the door, thinking it would be a delivery. Luath threw herself past me, and I knew who stood there.

I returned to the table where my headset and laptop were set up for work.

She whined and licked while he stroked her, then he stood at the table by me.

"When are you coming home?"

"No plans to."

"You can't go to school from here."

"I'll go somewhere else."

"Why? You already live right by the school you're set to attend."

Luath ran to me, wagging, nudging my arm, telling me with many exclamation marks Archer was here to see us.

"Why did you only start caring about me once I was blind?" I asked.

"What?"

"You were lukewarm for years. Once I was blind it was all, 'Won't you come live with me, Noah? Isn't this great? How about a vacation? How about getting married?' What the hell?"

"Maybe I just needed you to back off." The shock left his voice and he sounded angry. "Did you ever think of that? No. Never. Because it's all about *you*. I was shit-scared coming out to my family, okay? It's not like you—just floating by. When I moved here, I had no one. No one but you and them. I wasn't about to throw one away for the other. But we grew up and you stopped being so damn pushy. Then when I went to school—being away from you was terrible. I finally had to admit to myself I loved you." His tone bristled with hostility as he went on. "It had *nothing* to do with your damn eyes. Just come home."

"So you can take care of me? Tell me if my socks are mismatched and drive me to appointments and let me know if I've missed shaving cream on my face? Be saddled with me for the rest of your life? You've made it perfectly clear how selfish you find me. This is it. You're twenty-three. You can find a normal boyfriend."

"I *have* a normal boyfriend, except for his pigheadedness and unconventional word choices. I've already met the person I want to be with for the rest of my life. Do you honestly think mismatched socks are a deal-breaker?"

"This isn't funny, Archer."

"Isn't it? In a stupid, pointless way?"

"Go. Move on."

"Why is that *your* decision?"

"You asked. I said no."

"Then don't marry me, but come home anyway. This isn't one-sided. You dragged me into this relationship, and here I am. I need you no less now than when I was fifteen and sick with grief and you were the only person in the world who asked if I wanted to hang out. I want to hang out with you, Noah. Forever. Come home."

My chest hurt. My head hurt. My closed fists trembled in my lap. Never had I wanted sight more than at that moment.

"No," I whispered.

Summer blazed a blistering trail into August. School loomed

closer. I couldn't go, but I sat and sulked and never made the call to withdraw.

I hadn't heard from Archer since April. Maybe things were getting better for him. Maybe he'd met someone or was at least thinking about dating, going out with friends.

Something heavy dropped onto the couch beside me. I jumped.

"Sorry," Shiloh said. "I figured you heard me coming down the stairs."

I heard everything. Why hadn't I heard her?

She sighed and flipped on the TV.

"How was work?" I asked.

"Like you care."

I leaned away.

She flipped through channels for several minutes, then turned it off with another sigh. "God, you're stupid, Noah. I wish he'd asked me. What do you want? A fucking white horse?" She got up and walked away.

Luath and I listened to her go in silence.

I lay awake that night, clutching my old, private sketchbook, eyes closed, pretending I would open them to see Archer in the rain. I imagined I could see him beside me in bed, lying with my head on his chest, listening to his heart, kissing my way up his neck to his lips, though he didn't like it. He'd always been touchy about his neck. He put up with me. He let me rest my fingertips against his lips while he spoke so I could see him talking. He took pictures of Luath for me to email to her puppy raisers in California with detailed letters of her life and progress. He let me pick the carryout, or ate whatever I managed to cook, even the more suspect dishes. He gave me sight with his words, turned blank canvases into vivid paintings.

The next day, Saturday, once more alone with my dog, I called a cab.

Duffel bags in hand and Luath in harness, I walked across the sidewalk to our little condo. She paused. I lifted my foot to the step. We stopped on the landing.

I reached to feel the door and knock. I had a key in my pocket, but felt I'd lost that privilege. I swallowed and waited, sweat breaking out on my neck and palms. Luath's body vibrated as we listened to footsteps approach from inside. As hard as she wagged her tail, I knew she would never break her stance beside me without a release command to greet him.

The door opened.

Would he be willing to listen? Would he accept an apology? Would this even be him opening the door? Maybe another man who'd been over for Friday night? What would I say? Why hadn't I thought this through? One word from Shiloh and I came running back after all those months? Stupid. Not thinking.

Archer threw his arms around me.

I dropped the bags and harness to hug him, shaking, ribs crushed by his arms and chest.

Luath stood against my left leg, tail and whole back end swinging.

"I'm so sorry," I whispered. "Yes. If the offer still stands."

He kissed me, hands on my face, fingers in my hair, body pressed against mine on the narrow landing. He stepped back, still holding my head, and kissed me again.

When I released Luath, she sprang at him, whimpering. Archer knelt to hug her.

FALLING

James Booth

I have a feeling I'm going to regret tonight. Not for any big reason, like I'm going to kill somebody or hook up with a stranger I met online. It's so mundane—sneaking out to a party that'll just be the same old same old. But somehow my friend Taylor talked me into it, so here I am tiptoeing downstairs. Some of my friends sneak out through their windows; I don't need to do that. I wait for my parents to fall asleep, then go downstairs and out the family room door. So simple and it doesn't require any acrobatics.

I'm set to meet Taylor, Owen and Jane a block away from my house, where they'll drop me back off after the party. I go around the house to the lit neighborhood road and head to the meeting place.

Taylor's car races toward me as I stand on the corner. She stops in front of me. "Hey sexy, looking for a ride?" She's leaning across Owen to lasciviously stare at me while arching her eyebrows.

"Definitely, but it's gonna cost you!" I say, opening the back door and sliding in next to Jane.

Taylor holds up a couple of pennies. "This is all I've got."

"Eh, I'm cheap. I'll take it." I don't actually take the pennies though. What the heck would I do with those?

Owen has had enough of our game. "Come on guys. Let's get going."

"He just wants to get there so he can talk to Maya," Jane says, playfully slapping him on the arm. Despite his protests, I'm sure Owen's blushing, even though it's too dark to see.

"Justin, I heard there's gonna be some people from another school there tonight. Maybe there'll be a cute guy for you to chat up," Taylor says, while turning the car around and heading out of my neighborhood.

"First off, you say that every time and it's always the same people. Secondly, even if it were true, do you think I'd have the guts to go say hi to a cute boy? My gaydar sucks, too, so I don't want to flirt and then end up being punched. With my luck, you know that would happen."

"You never know. At least this party's near the waterfall, so even if a cute gay boy doesn't show up, there's that. It'll look pretty at nighttime." It's not exactly the best consolation prize. I'd rather have someone tell me I look pretty. Or, well, handsome. Whatever.

We arrive at the party, and it's already in full swing. It's almost a full moon out so there's not a huge need for extra lights, but I can see there's a fire going and some cars have their headlights on to illuminate the woods. Surprisingly, there are new people here from other nearby high schools. The party info must have been more widespread than I thought. Taylor gives me an *I told you so* look before heading to the keg to grab cups of beer for us. I'm not a big drinker, but sipping the beer at least gives me something to do.

I chat with my friends for a while, but eventually they all drift away to other people and I'm left wandering the party alone. I can hear the soothing flow of the waterfall in the distance and walk toward it.

Moonlight snakes through the tree branches and glitters off the water, giving it a dreamlike quality. I set my beer down on a nearby rock and pull off my shoes and socks, then roll up my pants so I can dip my legs into the water. It's an extremely peaceful moment and I close my eyes, breathing in the light woodsy smell. I am calm.

A twig snaps somewhere behind me and I become alert, swiveling to see who it is, causing water to splash onto my thighs. I stare at the most gorgeous boy I've ever seen. He looks a bit startled and also embarrassed.

"I didn't mean to spook you. I probably should've said something. Sorry." His hand brushes through his spiked black hair.

I realize that I have to say something, but I'm no good when it comes to dealing with guys, much less extremely hot ones. "I—it's okay," I stammer. Wow. What a brilliant display of the English language.

The guy comes closer and points to the spot beside me. "Is it all right if I join you?" I'm able to get out a yes, but my mouth clamps shut afterward. He takes off his shoes and socks but doesn't have to roll up anything since he's wearing shorts. I'm the idiot who wears pants even in summer; shorts expose my hairy legs. He, however, has smooth legs and I feel embarrassed by my own, which is such a stupid way to react. They're just legs, for crying out loud. But I feel insecure about my body.

"What brings you all the way out here?" he asks, gently swishing his feet through the water and looking over at me. I kind of huddle into myself thinking of an answer but may as well be honest about it.

"I got separated from my friends and decided to hang out here for a bit. Parties involving beer aren't really my thing." I shrug. "What about you? Shouldn't you be living it up with everyone else?"

"If I was back there, I wouldn't be with you," he nonchalantly replies. I glance at him with a little bit of suspicion, but I can see in his eyes that he's being truthful and not malicious or joking.

"Really?" I say, and he nods. "You don't know anything about me."

"I know you're cute and I'd like to get to know you better. That seems like a good start." He gives me a small smile. "Are you thinking the same things?"

Honestly, I'm still trying to grasp the fact that there's another gay guy at this party and that he's interested in me. Or at least interested in how I look, since we don't know each other. But he wants an answer. I smile. "Yeah, that would be nice."

He instantly relaxes and leans back on his hands. "I'm Dylan. I go to Bishop Becket High."

It's a private school about twenty minutes away.

"I'm Justin. I'm a senior at River Ridge."

"I'm a senior, too," he says.

"So you wear uniforms, huh? I bet you look really cute in yours." Oh my god, what just came out of my mouth? Was that *flirting?*

Dylan blushes, but he doesn't miss a beat and asks, "Have a thing for Catholic schoolboys?"

Now it's my turn to blush. I can't believe this is even happening—an actual conversation with a cute boy who's into me.

I'm about to reply with a maybe, but he places his hand on my leg. Even though it's hot out, I can feel the heat of him through my pants and I get a little excited. He looks serious. I'm wondering what he's going to say.

"I'm glad I came here tonight. I wasn't looking forward to it, but from the moment I saw you, I wanted to get to know you. I hope that's not too forward of me."

My surprise must be apparent on my face because he immediately backpedals.

"I'm sorry. I shouldn't have said that so soon. I always take things too fast and get too excited about a prospective guy. I'm so—"

I cut him off by putting my hand on his knee. I can feel his smooth warm skin. His embarrassment and similar insecurities help me find my own words.

"Hey, it's okay. I was thinking the same thing. I didn't think anything would happen tonight, but here we are. We can definitely keep getting to know each other." I want to kiss him, but I feel like now might not be the right time, so I quickly move on. "Tell me more about yourself."

He tells me that while he goes to a Catholic school, he's not Catholic anymore. He doesn't see any religion as having much base in his life. He has a cat named Hershey who's extremely fat and who he lovingly calls Hefty Hershey. He does choir, and though I pester him, he won't sing for me. I share with him that I do stage crew, feel an immense love for anime, and have an older sister in college in Idaho.

As we tell more about ourselves, we relax until we're leaning closer together, our hands still on each other's legs. No one even bothers to text or look for us, which is simultaneously sad and awesome.

Eventually we stop talking and just enjoy each other's

company, staring at the waterfall and listening to the sounds of the woods and the distant party. Dylan pulls back after a little while. "Do you wanna swim for a bit? There's a deeper section closer to the waterfall."

We're not wearing swim trunks and I know what that means—stripping down to our underwear. I don't know if I'm ready for him to see me like that. It's dark but still light enough to see each other's semi-naked bodies.

Still, he has spent all this time with me. I'm not exactly wearing a baggy shirt or anything, so he should know what my body type is. If he had a problem with it, he would've left by now.

"Sure." We strip off our shirts and pants, leaving us both in boxers. Even though I know he's gay and he's looking at me openly, I only sneak a peek at him as if I'm doing something naughty. He has toned abs and tanned skin, as opposed to me. I'm not fat or anything, but I have no definition. I'm pale, and I hope the moonlight reflecting off my skin doesn't blind him.

Dylan doesn't say a word as he walks into the creek. I follow him. Despite the heat of the night, the water is cold. It feels good as we go farther in. I'm cautious about where I step and almost crash into him when he suddenly stops and turns around. He stares at me intently and wraps his strong arms around me, making sure there's no gap between us. I look back at him, at the moonlight reflected in his eyes, and he leans in to give me the most perfect first kiss.

Yeah, I don't think I'm gonna regret tonight after all.

THANKSGIVING

Shawn Anniston

We met at a car wash. I probably wouldn't have given him a second look—too young and not a physical type I'm normally attracted to—except for his dog. I was sitting on a bench outside the squat, many-windowed building with my black Lab, Archie. I was thinking, as I probably had every day since adopting Archie from a shelter three years before, how strange it was that a low-key man like me had ended up with a high-energy dog. I knew Archie would love nothing more than for me to drop the leash so he could run through the spray of water, trying to bite it, shaking it from his coat and dancing back for more.

It was Archie's frantic tail wagging that first drew my attention to a dog a few benches away. I scrutinized him: mostly Great Pyrenees, I thought, because of the white coat, but his smaller stature betrayed him as a mixed breed. He sat motionless, staring over the busy lot with calm detachment.

"You could learn a thing or two from that one," I said to

Archie, shortening his lead before he could greet the woman who dropped to the other end of my bench. I sensed that she wasn't a dog person and wouldn't welcome Archie's slobbery gesture of friendship.

I looked back at the white dog, and then I let my gaze travel up to his companion. Earbuds connected him to his phone, on which he seemed to be furiously texting or playing a game. There was a Starbucks cup and an iPad next to him. From time to time, he picked up one or the other, while one Chuck Taylor-clad foot kept time with whatever he was listening to. Although I had as many or more gadgets, I felt my usual twinge of superiority at how I refused to be a slave to technology. I'd long ago amended an old saying to *Life is what happens while you're busy with your iProducts.*

At that moment, the man's head lifted, his gaze fell on Archie and he grinned. I knew his next move would be to judge me the way I'd been judging him, so I turned my head as if to watch the crew finish detailing my car, though I knew it wasn't on the lot yet. After sufficient time had passed for him to evaluate and dismiss me, I looked at him. Our eyes locked.

This is new, I thought as my heart felt a little jolt.

I stood, intending to go back inside the building as if it had just occurred to me that I needed a restroom or a bottle of water or a shoeshine. Except the man stood, too. The dogs began walking toward each other as if spotting an old friend, and we passively allowed ourselves to be pulled along behind them.

Eight years earlier, I'd purchased my loft in a midtown building with a great view of the city skyline. The neighborhood had everything I needed, and my office was only a short walk away. Ultimately that had been a good thing, because work was my escape. The loft came to feel like a cell of hard surfaces: gleaming granite and tile and bamboo. My friends loved it for parties, but no one would call it cozy.

It hadn't felt like home until Archie arrived, his toenails scratching the polished floors, tufts of his hair eluding the Roomba to roll into hidden corners and under furniture.

The first time Matthew brought his Great Pyrenees, Lionel, over for a playdate with Archie, his only word upon looking around was "shiny."

Nights we spent together were at his place: a three-bedroom apartment in a midcentury building where his two roommates tended to leave clothes draped over the furniture, dishes in the sink and Solo cups half-full of Diet Coke and soggy cigarette butts on the tiny patio.

It reminded me of my long-ago life as a college student. I tried not to analyze why I felt at home there or why I had no interest in introducing Matthew to my friends.

"At Mister Car Wash," my best friend Cory said, when I rejoined society several weeks later.

"Yep," I said, already regretting that I'd shared even that little.

"You've been, what, in bed with this Matthew guy ever since? This is why you don't return emails, texts or calls? This is why you missed the HRC gala?"

"I haven't—I didn't—not exactly," I said gracelessly.

"You *did* miss it," Cory insisted.

I thought his boyfriend Danny had been preoccupied with the menu, but he suddenly gave me a hard stare and said, "What do you mean, 'not exactly'? You haven't had sex? Or you don't want to talk about it? That would mean it's serious."

"Don't be crazy," Cory said. "We always talk about it. And of course there's been sex; those tickets he didn't use were three hundred each. Why didn't you bring him? Does he lack table manners? Does he have a mustache?" He shuddered. Facial hair repelled and excited him.

"There was a conflict," I said, and reached for Danny's menu. I wasn't sure why either of us needed it; our orders never varied at these occasional Sunday brunches.

"What kind of conflict?" Cory asked.

"Gallery opening Matthew had to attend," I said, focusing on a garish photo of eggs Florentine as if it were the latest cover of *Men's Health* magazine.

"He's an *artist?* No wonder you don't want to talk about him. It's okay. Order your whole-wheat waffle and we'll never speak of this again."

"If only that were true," I muttered.

"The best thing about Saturdays at your place," Matthew said, looking out from my tiny balcony, "other than the view, is how easy it is to walk to everything. Market, movies, museums. It's a very *M* world here."

"As it should be for Midtown," I said.

And Matthew, one side of my brain whispered.

Moving too fast, the other side nagged.

"You're ashamed of him," Sophia said sagely, as she watered the plants in my office.

Sophia is fifty-seven, and I suppose because she never had children, she'd decided to raise me. I finally gave up trying to impress on her that ours is a professional relationship—*You're my* assistant; *I have a mother; I can get my own coffee; I don't eat sweets; I'm forty-one; we pay a service to water our plants*—none of these have changed our dynamic through the years at Miller, Wheeling and Espy.

"I'm not ashamed of him," I said automatically.

"You didn't tell your friends because you'd rather they think you're dating an artist than a receptionist. An artist can be poor but his work is intriguing. A receptionist is underpaid and how many male receptionists do you know?"

"*Our* receptionist isn't underpaid."

"Ha!"

I'd never thought *Ha!* should be an actual spoken word so I pretended to read the contract in front of me.

"It's disappointing after all these years to find out how you really feel about support staff." I didn't look up or answer. "I guess it's a good thing I never went out with Mr. Wheeling or Mr. Espy."

"It is. Since Mr. Wheeling is married and Mr. Espy is a serial divorcé."

"Make jokes. The only things you hide from your closest friends are the things you're ashamed of."

"I'm not planning to move in or redecorate," Matthew assured me one Sunday afternoon when he arrived at my loft with his arms full of plants. Lionel pushed past him to greet Archie.

"I don't have a green thumb," I warned. "What if Archie eats the plants?"

"They're low maintenance and will be on the balcony," Matthew said. "Besides, I wouldn't bring anything that isn't dog friendly."

I shrugged and walked ahead of him to open the balcony doors.

"You could go back down with me and help me lug up the pots and planters," Matthew suggested.

It all felt like a very couple thing to do, and I tried to decide if I liked that while Lionel nudged me for an ear rub and Archie followed Matthew outside.

* * *

"I don't think you owe *anyone* all the details about a new relationship," Jennifer said, as she ran her hands over Archie's hind legs. She happened to be a close friend as well as his vet.

"Finally: someone sensible," I said.

"It doesn't matter what you tell them anyway. Most people only see things through their own lenses. Cory's a sex-crazed social climber. Sophia's insecure about her profession. Or maybe her importance in your life."

She patted Archie on his rump and smiled at the mad wagging of his tail when she reached inside the treat jar.

"I'm not even sure it *is* a relationship," I said. "He's just a man whose company I enjoy. Who happens to be a few years younger. Why does everyone have to analyze it?"

"I know! Why *do* people do that?" She looked through Archie's paperwork and said, "Archie's doing great. We'll see him again in six months. He'll be due for his rabies booster then."

As she walked me toward the reception area, she gave a little laugh and said, "Anyone who really knows you and Archie gets it."

"Gets what?"

"You're attracted to a man who's like your dog. You're a serious man with a frisky dog. He and his dog are the reverse. I see it all the time: people trying to compensate for their perceived deficiencies when seeking a companion animal or a mate."

Not that you're analyzing it, I thought.

By the end of summer, we were as likely to spend nights at my loft as his apartment. At my place, the plants were thriving. At his place, the roommates were starting to drop hints that maybe they should start looking for someone to replace him.

But neither of us seemed inclined to make changes beyond

the ones that happened gradually. On weekends, we wandered through galleries and he helped me pick out a few paintings for my bare walls. We tossed tennis balls at the dog park for Archie and Lionel. If we went to a movie or a restaurant, we no longer worried about who paid for what.

Although Matthew became less absorbed with his gadgets, and I spent less time at the firm, I occasionally liked to do my own research at the law library. Matthew enjoyed going with me, settling into a chair to read while I worked. One night I realized I'd been staring at a law review article for nearly half an hour without any idea what it said. I extended my leg to nudge Matt's foot under the table. He glanced up and grinned, then looked back at his iPad.

I love him. And chasing after that revelation: *Nothing that's expected to last can be this easy. Can it?*

I was chopping onions for my mother's tomato sauce while I tried to express the jumble of emotions and anxieties about where Matthew and I were headed.

She reached over, removed the knife from my hands, and said, "Nope."

"What?" I looked at the onion. "I'm cutting it the way I always have."

"I'm not talking onions. Neither are you. You're forty-one."

"Your point is..."

"He's thirty-two. This sounds suspiciously like a midlife crisis. Next comes the overpriced sports car. This is your father's department. He's in the garage." She saw my exasperated expression. "Staring helplessly under the hood of that stupid Dodge Challenger."

"Charger," I corrected her.

"See? It's a man thing. You two can bond over it. Go."

I glanced back as I walked into the laundry room, but Archie refused to look away from the woman moving around the kitchen, the potential source of far more delights than anything the garage could offer.

"Make sure he doesn't get any of that onion," I reminded her, but she only waved me out.

My father had one of the bay doors up, but he wasn't looking under the hood of the Charger, which wasn't his car anyway. It had been a project of my younger brother's, abandoned unfinished as so many were, and left to take up space in my parents' garage. Like the workout equipment still in my brother's bedroom, it had become a surface for the random detritus of the lives going on around it.

My father had turned the garage into his version of a man cave, a place where he could smoke his skinny cigars, kick back in his decades-old recliner that had been banished from the house and read. Today it was a *Rolling Stone* with another barely legal, barely dressed singer on the cover. If my mother was right about my midlife crisis, was my father a warning that it could last a few more decades?

He pointed his beer toward the garage refrigerator to let me know they were there if I wanted one.

"Ma sent me out so you could help me navigate male menopause." I opened my beer and unfolded a lawn chair, facing it toward the street rather than him.

He grunted, put the magazine aside, and said, "If you're looking for an impractical car, I'm sure your brother would sell you that one."

"No, thanks. Apparently my only symptom is that I'm seeing a younger man."

"Does this younger man have a name?"

"Matthew. Matt."

"Details," he said, giving me the fierce stare that had once made even the most seasoned prosecutors wish they could exit the courtroom.

I gave him the rundown, including the opinions of everyone who'd offered them since I'd met Matthew.

My father got us both another beer, settled into his chair and then said, "Let me see if I have this right. He's a receptionist, but you don't work in the same place. You're not his boss."

"Right."

"So no sexual harassment. You make more money than he does. Has he stolen your credit cards? Hacked into your bank account? Hit you up for money?"

"Of course not."

Another grunt. "You get along with each other's dogs? They get along with each other?"

"I'm not sure this is helping. Instead of giving me fatherly advice about Matthew, you're making me question the wisdom of my friends, my assistant, and my vet."

"I don't think the difference of a few years or a few dollars is a big deal," he said.

"Yeah, but what if—"

"Here's your fatherly advice. You can't think like a lawyer in love."

"That magazine is doing you no good if your musical references are almost as old as me."

"Bring him for Thanksgiving."

Thanksgiving was the High Holy Day in our family. We could miss birthdays, anniversaries, even Christmas if we'd made other plans, but all children and grandchildren were expected to be in their appointed chairs at the table on the fourth Thursday of every November.

"I appreciate the offer, but Thanksgiving is, like, three months from now," I said. "Who knows whether—"

"You should warn him that we don't like any cranberry sauce except the kind with the can lines on it. Though I doubt anything so trivial could derail a relationship."

I sat back with my beer. After a minute, my father picked up his *Rolling Stone* and I felt a stupid grin settle on my face.

THE INVINCIBLE THEATRE

Felice Picano

A theatrical troupe arrived unannounced in Covent Garden late one very breezy afternoon when all of us were going starkers chasing after our bonnets, hats, cash boxes and stray stalks of airborne gladiolus.

The actors clangorously trundled into the square within two large, overblown, colorful, horse-drawn caravans and immediately camped at the far northeastern corner, where infrequent entertainment customarily set up stage.

The latter had, during my time there so far, been constituted of: a wagon full of cheerless, flyblown marionettes in so-called dramatizations of old legends that even the youngest disdained as puerile. I also recall an ancient Punch and Judy Show from somewhere in Essex, last costumed and painted up in the time of King George Second. Most recently, we'd been treated to a family dance company from Scotland purporting to be "Hebrides-bred and authentikal," about which the less said, the better for any future intercourse with our northern neighbor.

MONSIEUR GUILLAUME DARROT AND THE INVINCIBLE THEATRE read the man-sized placards of the new troupe, stood on either side of the little stage that was quickly erected between ends of two high-sided caravans parked six yards apart in the corner. Handbills distributed by myself, as a hired lad, named the individuals of the company, which besides M. Darrot, included Madame Suzette Darrot; Mademoiselle Antoinette Genre; M. De Sang Pur—doubtless the large, bearded, bald headed fellow I had noted moving large objects about so much—and a "Grande-Madame de St. Clement-En-Hors-de-Combat," whom we were assured would play roles deemed "Domestic, Deistic and Outlandish."

I laughed as hard as the other flower vendors, fruiterers and marrow-sellers, reading aloud for them this piece of Frenchified gallimaufry. Even so, two nights later I joined an audience of several score, requiting my ha'pence for the troupe's first performance: "The Most Despicable and Horrible Tragedy of the Tyrone Family of ____ County, Ireland—after a tale written by that estimable Mr. Joseph Bodin de Sheridan Le Fanu." And like the other threescore in the audience, I was terrified, frightened and moved. Moved so much, in fact, that four days later and after having seen every one of their performances, I resigned The Covent Garden, flower-selling, and the Hellenically-inclined Newholl family forever, and I joined the Invincible Theatre troupe.

M. Darrot turned out to be an individual no more exotic than a Mr. William Darrow, or Billy-Boy Dee, as his sire, another member of the troupe, one Jonathan Darrow (i.e., Mr. Pure Blood, or De Sang-Pur) called him. For all his age and considerable airs, Darrow the Elder was no more wellborn than your humble servant, My Lord, and hailed from some inconsequential townlet in Surrey. And the purity of his blood, if it ever existed, must do daily battle with prodigious amounts of gin and whiskey to discover which liquid would prevail.

Still, the old reprobate was docile and had been for many long moons an actor with other troupes, including what remained of The King's Men during the realm of the last Regent, and so he had memorized his acting parts, or at any rate had gotten several resonantly long speeches by heart.

It was those speeches that Darrow the Younger had pilfered, and around them had since begun to scribble his own plays, far more popular adaptations of our then-contemporary literature as found in various three-volume novels and periodicals, along with those foreign dramas he happened upon and then lifted wholesale. Add to those two or three expurgations of Mr. Shakespeare filled with blood, thunder, ghosts and revenge, and that was the troupe's entire repertoire.

The great female dramaturge of the company, Madame Suzette Darrot, was in fact Suzie Darrow, née Semple, wife to Billy-Boy. Mademoiselle Antoinette Genre was in truth her niece by blood, a Miss Amy Green. As for the fifth member of the company, it would be many months before I uncovered that remarkable personage's complete identity and rather odd verity.

Meanwhile, during their short engagement at the Covent Garden's out of doors corner, I had progressed with The Invincibles from being a mere set-up helper, to a placard boy, and on to becoming a constant "stage-handy lad," assisting Billy in setting up the changes of scenery. These commonly consisted of two parts: a painted background, or as they called it "rear scrim," and a variety of deal or other lightweight wood (and thus quite mobile) furniture upon which the actors would perch and lean for verisimilitude, though few might actually hold the full weight of the somewhat rotund Darrow Elder for longish periods of time. I also drew the curtains to open and close the show as well as to register the so-called Entr'actes.

An immediate fascination with their art attracted me into the circle of The Invincible Theatre. Growing knowledge and increasing appreciation of their craft and all it comprised, indeed required, drew me even more tightly into their tiny realm. Thence, a kind of juvenile passion with those two lovely—and one bizarre—women enmeshed me ever more approximate.

It was my total fixation upon Billy Darrow that at last folded me into the troupe's most intimate circle—for while I had before idolized members of the female sex, for the first time in my life, I found a male worthy of my uttermost infatuation.

Was he handsome then, this leading actor, you will ask, My Lord? Of course he was; he was a leading man of an acting troupe, after all. But then again, feature by feature, he was not especially remarkable. He had learned through stage makeup to over-benefit the advantages of his better facial features: his fine glittering black eyes he emphasized by further application of dark paint to his eyebrows and by thickening to ebony his eyelashes. His nose I knew for a fact at close sight to be slightly bent to the left. No matter, he painted a straight line down to its tip despite the bone, and shaded it from either side, and it appeared ferrule-straight. He re-limned and then daubed into the new outline his upper lip so it might be as voluptuous as its mate. He oh so softly rouged his cheekbones so they shone not quite so high, to make himself more cherubic for younger roles. Even so, later on, when a play-described "brilliant beau" was required for a walk-on role, Billy was the first to toss my own self, clad in gilt velvet with silver frogging, onto that never-very-steady movable stage in lieu of himself for the audience to ooh and ahh over. True his figure was slim and long, but he believed it almost simian, with his somewhat apelike long arms and large hands. His posture was never quite Royal, unless it must be for a role. No, he was ever an indifferent King, preferring always that his elder or even the mysterious and multi-named fifth member take over those majestic roles when they were of a short duration.

As compensation, Billy was, however, most lithe, most flexible and most assuredly athletic. He could juggle, he could somersault, he could leap high enough to make audiences gasp, and he would then just barely alight, one shaky foot atop a single shivering beam, his entire body vibrating as though he would topple over, and yet hold his ground steady—to everyone's amazed relief. In short, he could, with no trouble at all, incur every viewer's eye by a score of differing means and hold it—just as long as he wished. If his voice was nothing especial, a fair tenor, still he could sing several airs of Mr. Handel and Herr Mozart with perfect tone and pitch and he would leave a tear in your eye and a throb in your breast. But for the grand dramatic speeches, he must drag in that old sot, his sire, whose resounding baritone was a natal gift. As the lad Billy-Boy had watched his pater to learn, so watched I him every moment onstage, whether in rehearsal or on show, to educate myself into what turned out to be an only middling grasp of the actor's craft.

And if Billy Darrow was admirable, he was even more so when he had someone to admire him. By this tenth year of The Invincible Theatre's existence, that meant no one other than myself. His wife was by then quite inured; his father was, as always, uninterested; and who knew what the fifth member thought, as we only heard uttered speech onstage; even Billy's niece by marriage, his last conquest before me, was looking about for someone other to engage her esteem.

It was she, Miss Amy, who three months into my employment with the troupe, made the discovery that despite all my larking about London town, among some of its most unsavory haunts and disreputable gutters, I was still pure as the driven snow.

We had left London some week past and only just set up stage in the large, second common green of Sheffield town, and I had just returned from depositing our placards about those shop fronts that would countenance our adverts in their windows, when she faced me down. Her arms were akimbo, her chestnut hair all flying about, her cheeks reddened from proximity to the boiling hot water: in short, quite notably natural for once, and if I must say so, quite lovely, too. The scene was the outdoor fire where she and her aunt were laundering the troupe's clothing in preparation for the week to come. By this time I had come into a second set of shirt and trousers and so had given in my originals for cleansing.

"What's this then?" she asked pointing to a stain no more remarkable to my eye than any other, except perhaps its location, slightly above the *Y* of my trouser legs. As I looked, she looked me in the eye and said, "Jizz, is what. Look Ess, how he does stain himself at night."

I was unaware of staining myself at night or any other time and said so, unawares they were japing with me, until Mrs. Darrow asked, "Have you then no dreams at all, a lad your age, of ladies fair?" Upon which I blushed to recall one such dream about herself.

She laughed, but quickly enough the two of them calculated, and then asked, "Haven't you ever? With a lass or lady?" And what was I to say. I turned and fled, murmuring of some work that must be attended to immediately.

That night, my idol roused himself from his conjugal bed within Caravan Number One and came to where I had cobbled together my own more makeshift sleeping quarters on the street beneath Caravan Number Two.

"Come, my love," for that was how Billy spoke to all of us, my love, my darling, my sweetheart. "Come up to bed with Suzie and me."

I was to say the truth amazed, for the cobblestones were especially iron-hard with ice that night with autumn coming on, despite my many efforts to disguise them with slats and cloths; any softer lie-down would be preferable.

No sooner had we crept into the caravan and I was at the edge of the bed, viewing by faint candlelight Mrs. Darrow herself, all pink skinned, wrapped in warm covers atop softer pillows, then from behind, I felt his hands upon me. Before I knew what he was about, he'd stripped off my trousers and shirt and pushed me atop her. From there, she took over, and any questions I may have uttered were stilled by first her and then him. Soon were we all three as Nature made us, and almost as quickly was I between her large soft breasts, myself being fondled and kissed, manipulated and managed from in front and in back by one and the other simultaneously, until having found a wet harbor below and pushed to it, I found a rhythm and soon began to gasp. What heaven! Twice more did I consort with the distaff, while the husband consorted with the lady from behind, and alternately encouraged me with many caresses and lewd remonstrations. Through it all, I encountered and experienced so many differing sensations and emotions that when it was all over, and the three of us were at last spent to our utmost, I lay between them both, and murmured my double adoration, before I collapsed into utter debilitation.

Once having tasted such delights, how then was I to be denied? I was not. From then on, for months on end, I bedded with my master and my mistress. True it was that the lady tired of our frolics earlier some nights than the fellow did, and would fall asleep, leaving Darrow to divert me. Increasingly as I appeared,

I would in vain seek her and be told she was sharing Amy's bed that night. Or more simply, "Getting her much-needed sleep, for she worked hard today, two shows and three parts, and she knows she'll get little enough sleep with you about." Said sternly, just before Billy kissed my lips and rifled my undergarments with his monkey-quick hands.

In vain did I attempt to draw Miss Amy into our nocturnal diversions. "Leave her be, the poor thing," Suzie would exclaim. "Haven't she enough of men folk during the day!" This latter not so much directed at myself, who outside of the bed at Caravan One remained as shy and diffident as before; nor did it refer to our leader, much as I would come upon him all unawares staring at the lass when she knew not he was about, and he surely appeared to have more than theatrical ambitions upon his mind.

No, but it did allude to Mme. Genre's slow but certain new appearance, her growth, both physical and dramatic, lending her far greater stature and her experience, providing greater repute, so that when his wife complained of too much labor, our Billy-Boy simply transferred the roles to his niece. Amy took them on with a loud enough grumble and a demand for "more meat and less gristle," but despite these noises, in truth she took on the new parts joyfully and acquitted herself very well indeed.

So well that she acquired admirers. Indeed, by the time we had arrived as far as Nottingham Shire, Mme. Genre could rely upon several gentlemen's carriages to be parked just outside the circle that comprised our audience; the owners seated upon foldout seat-contraptions prepared by their valets or drivers, near enough to the stage where they might admire Amy from closer quarters—an advantage Darrow charged a half shilling for, per head. I would not have been amazed to have closed down in one town and set up for travel to another and seen our little tripartite retinue followed by another entire and quite longer cortege of Amy's guest-admirers.

"They used to follow *me* so," Suzie whimpered very early one morning when we had shared a bed together again, all three: she, I and Billy. The back curtains of the van formed a little *V* out which I could see the predawn constellation Cassiopeia clearly against the cobalt night. Her husband soothed her, holding her tight about as she sobbed on. "Even more admirers than she. Even higher born. Do you remember, Billy?" He did remember, loyal mate that he was and he said so, and they reminisced about Lord This and Baron That until she was mollified a bit, at which she caught sight of me and declared, "Does it never go down? I ask you, truly. Never? Ah, well, at least *one* handsome lad admires me," and turned to cover me with her soft form, and so I was forced to somewhat awaken, while Darrow added his own domestic admiration from behind her.

I mentioned triple 'vans because we had gained a third, somewhat smaller and older than the others and thus in a more parlous state, yet withal useful, because that's where Darrow the Elder, and the silent and apart from us but for the stage Fifth Troupe Member now slept and kept their costumes and other belongings, Suzie having moved many of hers to be with Amy. So I now had a home up off the cobblestones and while not my own bed, at least the first real example of such an object since I was an infant.

Partly this was ascribable to our increased "box-office" as the nightly monetary receipts were euphemistically spoken of, there being a box, if no office. Amy's new followers certainly were partly responsible for that boon, but so it turned out was I. For I soon became a performer in the troupe myself, and if I may be immodest, a not terribly unimportant addition to the company, especially to the lasses and women-folk, for by now

I, too, had grown almost as tall as Darrow and had sprung soft down upon my lip and cheek and chin, which Suzie and even Billy did fawn upon.

Even in the most stalwart of troupes, actors "go down"—get ill, or depressed, or vanish two days on end larking with some townsperson, or refuse to leave their caravan from "a case of the sulks."

Our fifth ordinarily silent troupe member was the first to become ill, with a catarrh that interfered mightily with her ability to speak sans a cough. She did lovely work of hiding it or stitching it into the scenes she played, just as though it belonged there. The first two nights, at least, she did. The third night it proved impossible for her to get out of bed or leave Caravan Three for her feverish state, and thus I was cast in her place.

The play was The Bard's *Tragedy of Romeo and Juliet* and the most unlikely part I was to take over for her was a small female role, that of Lady Montague, Romeo's mother, with but a handful of lines. The largest role that I must slip into in her stead was that of Mercutio, playing to Billy as my best friend. I had learned by heart the two speeches already: one fantastical and the other pathetic. Later on, I was to play gruff Friar Laurence, and what lines I was unsure of would be whispered to me by someone or other in the company, offstage at the time.

In the first role of the young smart, I japed much with Billy who played Romeo, and who in turn flirted back at me, giving a new significance to these young men's close friendship in the play. This impelled one Oxonian within the audience to laugh out loud and call, "Why, look! They are as *Greek* as ever were *Italian lads*! And I'll wager as prompt at each other with their *cods* as with their *daggers!*"—a comment that earned much merriment.

Later on, as the Friar, my beard did itch badly, as did my

monk's cowl, and I was eager to be rid of those, but the applause was delightful, and when Mercutio was called for, I vanished and reappeared sans beard and blanket but wearing the other's doublet and feathered hat, and bowed to even greater kudos.

Later that night, as we sat in the local public house gobbling down our late and by no means undercooked dinner, t'was Suzie who said of me, "He's bit. Why look. As surely as though it were a gadfly upon his neck, he's bit by the streaming limed-lamps he's fired up himself and by the yokels' hand claps—stage-bit, the great dolt!"

I colored deeply for it was not entirely untrue. Darrow Elder—who seldom spoke once his tankard was in hand—deigned to utter to me, "A capital Queen Mab, lad." Then pondering, he added, "A somewhat less creditable death speech." Which drove us to hilarity, for he could not give aught, not even words, but he must take something back, all the time.

After that night I remained onstage with The Invincible Theatre troupe, earning my own sobriquet, Monsieur Addison Aries, a name conjured by the Darrows, husband and wife, out of my own given name and an old Astrological Almanack one of the company had snitched somewhere in Northern Wales and which they followed closely, for they were a superstitious lot, all of them, our mysterious fifth actor included. None of the women stepped onstage without first spitting behind herself and twirling her index finger in a curlicue while uttering below her breath, "Pig's foot!" Though none could tell from whence it all derived.

And so, My Lord, I passed my thirteenth, fourteenth and fifteenth birthdays as Mercutio and Tybalt, as Friar Laurence and Lady Montague, as Lord Marchmell and the Duke of Tickles, as Raggs the Sheep-herd and Stiggs the Scrivener, as Charles Surface, and Young Dornton, as Captain Absolute (to Billy's seductive Catesby) and Sir Derleth Tyrone the Younger, as

Doctor I. M. A. Dandy and Mlle. Camille du Sprech, as Young Fool and Old Liar, as Unknown Bandit, and First Soldier, once even as Lord Beverley, and twice as Lord Mayor of London; but in short as a repertoire-actor. For Billy Darrow was no fool and knew that whatever extra I earned from him on the boards I soon brought in trebled in farthings, quickly gaining for that new Invincible troupe actor, M. Aries his own little "claque," for so one's followers are named.

I was furthermore useful in so many other ways to his company: as stage worker, as tender lover to his wife, who thus minded less her usurpation in the company by her niece and so didn't make the expected trouble; and not least of all useful as Billy's own personal Antinous, for I was rich with spunk, and he was determined to mine it out of me one way or t'other.

I have mentioned before the fifth member of the Invincible Theatre. But have always done so mysteriously and for good reason: mysteriousness seemed to hover about this troupe member from morn till night and despite the greatest illumination thrown from a fire-lighted stage limelight.

This actor played both male and female. No surprise, when so did myself at different times, as did Amy Green. I have also said this actor possessed a voice of surpassing range. Singing from a higher soprano than Suzie Darrow down to bass notes that our senior-most fellow, old Jonathan Darrow, might—and regularly did in his speeches—encompass. They boarded together in one wagon, yet utterly apart; and it did not signify that anyone knew the better nor associated the more with this Theatrickal Enigma.

More than once did I ask Billy Darrow who this *Personne de Grand-Chance* might be, in truth.

"Leave it be, Addison, my love, for no good can come of your needing to know."

"But surely that person is not of the Darrow kith and kin?"

"That is so."

"Then how came this person to your troupe?"

"By slow degrees. By a downfall from a greater estate," Billy said.

We were pulling up stakes for the tented enclosure against poor weather that some folks paid a shilling extra for as we spoke, so I well recall our conversation. "But surely a smart lad like you has already discovered that for himself."

"You mean because of this person's great adaptability?"

"That, too. But mostly because who else among us can hold an audience so completely rapt?"

"Why yourself," answered I, ever loyal. "With your tumbles and leaps and tricks."

"Aye, that foolishness—and only betimes!"

"And your sire, too, with his tragic speeches."

"All five of them—when he chooses to be sober."

"And Miss Green, when she wears her bodice low upon her bust and flirts."

"And yourself for all that, when you are dressed in gold and well peruked and flirt with the ladies in the second row," he answered. "But surely you've noted how different our Great Person is?"

I had and yet could not put it into speech, and so I held my own.

"Do not be bothersome to any one in the troupe, Addison, or I shall have to whip you, too, among the many fleshly duties I already manage."

So was I warned.

By this time we had begun a new play, Mr. Shakespeare's *Twelfth Night*, much expurgated, naturally enough given our audiences and their general understanding, chopped back to no more than two hours, albeit full of wit and flirtation. None more so than between the maid Viola, dressed as a man to court the noble Olivia for Duke Orsino, and Olivia herself, who then mistakes Viola's stranded brother, Sebastian, for Cesario and forces him to wed her.

We had rehearsed this, myself as Sebastian for The Invincibles, but most of all playing opposite Suzie, with whom I had been second husband for nigh three or more years by now and with whom I felt most congenial.

All the more of a surprise then, when Amy came down with a rotten tooth and could not play the opening. An even greater surprise to myself that Suzie Darrow would then play Viola, a role she knew well, and that our fifth person then took over the role of Lady Olivia, evidently having been several roles in the play in previous years—or decades—I knew not which.

This I discovered only as I made the announcement of the parts and the cast before the curtain on opening day in a rather large market square at the town of Croydon.

Our mysterious fifth actor as Olivia flirted believably and also gave the part emotion, and even evoked tears on the cheeks of the females of the audience with her sad plight. More than one of them had loved a youth and not been loved in return.

I was astonished when she dropped all the reserve that had surrounded her with mystery and grasped my hand, clasped me about the body, stage whispered insinuating and lovingly, and then kissed me so deeply I thought I might lose my wits. Baffled I looked then—as fitted Sebastian in the play—but in reality, too. For one who had never before as much as regarded me, now seemed to have adored me from afar, and only just then allowed me to understand that fact. Rustlings among the front seats showed that they, too, had intuited the real passion exerted betwixt us two. From the back-most standees came low whistles and even a growl or two, marking me as a "lucky dog."

Nor was I physically released during the short scene behind the curtains but held ever more closely, with much hand fumbling about my person, so that I must stick out like some fool jackanapes did I not put my clothes in order in time for the final scene in which Viola and Sebastian are reunited and the Duke and she become as one, while Sebastian and Olivia again passionately and lovingly retroth their pledge and all exeunt, leaving Billy all alone onstage to sing, "When I was a tiny little boy, with a hey-ho, the wind and the rain."

Behind the curtains once again, I turned to our mysterious fifth player and said, "Tonight. At ten o'clock. Be certain old Darrow is dead drunk." She responded with a hand upon my manhood.

And so as the clapping endured and we two were especially applauded, was that stage that had been my life—and I do not at all mean that little makeshift stage that was The Invincibles Theatre—set for its next quite dramatic act and transformational scene.

How inflamed I was after that provincial premiere of Billy's expurgated *Twelfth Night* you may easily imagine. Seldom have I been quite so heated.

The hours I must wait dragged by like Eternity itself and it was all I could do to not drink myself ale-blind, as we four, Suzie, Billy, Jonathan and myself, celebrated our quite substantial take from our performance in a local pub, named—and this is one of those coincidences that makes my life so piquant—The Fallow Deer. Naturally Billy was looking forward to future performances as we were already the talk of the town, especially as several townsfolk stopped by our table and asked for a repeat the following night. More cheer followed that, you may be assured.

At last we all wandered away to our wagons, Jonathan drunk, Billy and Suzie cordially tipsy, and myself in a quiet frenzy of anticipation, albeit acting as though I, too, were inebriated.

So they pushed me into sick Amy's wagon, where she slept snoring away and none too clean smelling, while they celebrated with a rare husband and wife cohabitation.

As the 'vans were placed together in one side corner of a minor lane of the main square, I could, by peeping out of the curtains sometimes even see what took place in the other two. Thus, at ten o clock sharp—by the local steeple bells—I was on the flagstones outside the smaller van, as washed and close to undress as I dared be, making my whistle-signal to the *Grande Personne* herself.

Naturally the interior was dim-lit, a mere candle-end set upon a carton of costumes that served as a bed stand. Through the wooden partition, I could easily hear the stentorian gasps and wheezing, snores, and assorted harrumphs of old Jonathan in his sleep.

And there lay my Love, all soft and white skinned amid her furled bedclothes. Her hair lay in shining ringlets upon her noble neck, and tumbled a bit upon one ivory shoulder. I might easily make out the softly ridged concavity of her back, guarded as it was by her two pillowy softnesses. She turned an unpainted face toward me and with one finger, soubrette style, to her lips bade me be very quiet.

She lay like that as I removed my shirt and trousers—I'd come barefoot—as though musing, and she seemed most pleased, as she reached for my extremity that greeted her so avidly.

Soon enough I was atop her and fondling. Unlike Suzie or even Amy, she was slender rather than voluptuous, smooth skinned, free of that padding wherein I might lose myself after passion. Her breasts were small and almost firm but were as much her weakness as any other female once I had them well in hand. Soon enough was I hand-guided to her lower regions and there she equaled Suzie well enough.

As onstage, her kisses were intoxicating and I will even use the oft repeated term *breathtaking*. At times, I believed I might never recover my breath unless I detached myself from those avid lips. I did so less and less as she guided me within herself, and from atop and behind her I began my manly ministrations.

Believe me, My Lord, when I report I never had encountered before and seldom since, such passion from a partner in love-making. Most ladies merely *receive* a gentleman, some with greater motion than others, few with such enthusiasm and few with her (I thought of the words at the time) athleticism and unstanched hunger.

Quickly enough, despite my efforts, did we rise and fall toward that bliss that is common to all. Much as I resisted, much as I had been taught by Suzie and Billy Darrow to resist, all teaching went for naught in that bed. Nor were either of us satisfied even then, but we must start up again for a second time, and while that lasted longer and we rose to new feats of inter-twining, never mind conclusion, even that did not suffice—but we must try a third time.

If I seem somewhat muddled in the telling now, My Lord, you may well imagine how utterly befuddled with longing and lust was I at the time. And so I shall attempt to write it as I recall, precisely and in order.

Firstly, we had risen off the mattresses, such as they were, and now were standing up, my mistress holding on to the curbed upper bars of the caravan for support, myself holding on to her chiefly and every once or twice in a while, also grasping an over-head strut.

As I was riding my way into my final *voyage de amour*, one

hand cupping her small breast slid downward; to it I joined my second hand and just as the great heat was upon me, it slipped farther down and encountered—how can I write it?—manhood as large and stiff as my own! Yes, right there, inches above a distinct womanhood.

I gasped quite loudly. At the same time, I felt myself drawn in ever more deeply, and closely. She spent. I spent. And all the while I had one hand on her manhood and another upon her womanhood.

In that same instant the partition shook and splintered and Jonathan Darrow himself, wide awake and bulging red with drink thundered, "Must you? Must you? Must you yet again?"

His complaint was stopped by the vision that even a vat of ale and a decanter full of Scots Whiskey could not undo: the vision that is, of ourselves, standing before him *in flagrante* and possessing not two but instead three sets of genitals!

"What then," he stammered. "What demons be ye?" he added, doubtless quoting lines from some play we knew not. And fell over the partition and onto the bed alongside us.

My companion pulled free of me and leapt to the bit of floor where clothing was tossed all about until some semblance of costume was put on. I stood there I fear in great astonishment, clad as I was the minute I was born. Old Jonathan rose in his fusty bedclothes and lurched toward me. I fought him down and rushed out the 'van following my partner who, now dressed, had alighted and stood in a defending posture, looking like Achilles in those prints by Mr. Flaxman.

Roused by the great noise, Billy and Suzie and even Amy had looked out of their curtains just as Jonathan tumbled out of the 'van after me and lunged toward me, only to be stopped by a perfectly aimed and quite powerful full-fisted blow to the nose by—not I—but *my lady transformed into man.*

He howled in pain, and soon those in the pub's inn chambers nearby had thrust up their window sashes and the scene was there for all to see.

My hermaphrodite pushed past me once more into the 'van and thrust my clothing at me where it fell upon the cobbles, and in a minute she—or he?—had run to the front exit, leapt onto one of the old bays kept there unshafted, and roused it with a kick. Minutes later we witnessed our fifth actor riding upon it, bareback as any American Indian or Amazon warrioress, off across the square of Croydon and rapidly into the frosty night.

By this time the entire plaza and surrounding streets were lighted up as I pulled on my trousers. Folks were shouting and calling jibes at us, and throwing down objects upon our heads.

"Damn your hot blood!" Billy Darrow shouted and rushed out at me. "Didn't I tell you *not to*?" Luckily he stumbled in his ill-timed charge at me.

In short time I was up and inside, past Suzie and gathering my belongings and hidden pay. I was upon the ground again in time to hear Billy railing, "You've ruined everything. Everything! Everything!"

Still not fully clad, I pushed on my shoes as best I could, blew Suzie a kiss and then I, too, sped off on foot in the direction of the most surprising lover of my life. Although toward where exactly, and what I expected to find, I could not say.

CARVER COMES HOME

Rob Byrnes

Carver DeMaris guides his rental car off I-76 and makes a right at the intersection a few miles from the house he lived in for the first seventeen years of his life. Twenty-one if you count intermittent breaks from college. He only counts the first seventeen.

He passes familiar sights. The high school, with a sign out front still congratulating the seniors who graduated months earlier. The post office, one lonely car parked next to the flagpole. Cookley Park, the grass short and brown in the August heat.

He turns left onto a wider road. A succession of signs dominate the view: McDonald's, Arby's, Dairy Queen, Village Inn, Sonic, Burger King. They used to call it Fast Food Alley. Maybe they still do.

At the light past the Burger King, before the traffic backup waiting to enter the Walmart parking lot, Carver makes another turn. A half-mile down the road he passes a peeling sign—"Welcome to Patience: It's a Virtue"—and the car bumps over a set of railroad tracks poking through crumbling pavement.

There's no need to slow down. Patience—in the flat eastern plains of Colorado—hasn't seen a train for a long time.

A few more turns and he spots the white clapboard house. The hedges are overgrown.

He's home.

His sister's Lexus is in the driveway, so new it still bears dealer plates from a Denver auto showroom. He parks behind it, grabs a small suitcase from the backseat and walks toward the rear of the house. Three wooden steps lead to a side door—there's also a front door no one ever uses—but he passes them and continues to the backyard.

The lawn needs attention, but his mother's marigolds look healthy, vibrant even, in the growing shadows. There's not a lot about Patience to miss, but he'll miss those marigolds.

Carver lets himself inside the house through the unlocked door into the kitchen. He lets his eyes adjust to the light, taking in familiar objects in the gloom of early evening. Ceramic bears on the stovetop with SALT and PEPPER printed on their bellies. An inspirational calendar held to the refrigerator with magnets. A wicker basket on the round table, overflowing with circulars from the Patience Price-Cut Market. The crucified Christ, arms extended across the wall beneath a clock that was never set to Daylight Saving Time.

He's home, but he's not. This really isn't home anymore.

A *click click click* approaches, hard heels against hardwood.

"I *thought* I heard someone down here." His sister Julie flicks the light switch and gives him a brief welcoming hug. She takes after their father, dark and short. He's their mother's son, fair and tall. "Carver DeMaris has come home. Let the party begin!"

He smiles at her irreverence and glances at the ceiling, in the vague direction of his mother's bedroom. "How's she doing?"

Julie shakes her head. "Dr. Hamilton gives her another day or two."

"Dr. Hamilton? He's still alive?"

"Tick tock."

Carver glances back at the ceiling. "Is Mom awake? Can I see her?"

"She's sleeping. But when she's awake, she's alert. Well, alert enough to know you're there."

"Do you think she'll wake up again tonight?"

"Who knows? This can wait, though, right?"

"Maybe not."

Julie's left eyebrow arches. "Can't it wait until she's feeling up to it?"

He leans back against the linoleum counter. "She's not getting better than she is right now." She nods, but won't make eye contact. "I need to talk to her before she goes."

"Drama queen." Julie says this almost under her breath, but not quite. He's sure she wanted him to hear.

"What was that?"

Finally, she can look him in the eye. "I don't need any more drama, Carver. I'm stressed to the max as it is."

He clears his throat. "Speaking of that 'queen' thing..."

Julie has always had an uncanny ability to finish his unspoken thoughts. It's clear she isn't happy. "Suddenly it occurs to me that *this* is what you desperately have to tell our mother."

He looks away. His eyes find the salt and pepper bears. "We have some unfinished business."

"Don't. I don't need this. And she's probably past the point of understanding."

"But..."

"What are you trying to accomplish here, Carver?" She looks

around distractedly until she spots her purse on the counter between the toaster and a cutlery block. "I need a cigarette. Want one?"

"Of course not."

"Then come outside and watch me." Julie picks up the purse and walks out the side door and down the three steps to the driveway, not waiting for Carver to answer. He follows. He always does.

"Bad habit," says Carver.

"I didn't ask you. Better people than you have told me that, and I didn't ask *them*, either." Julie inhales and exhales immediately. "So, Mom's about to die and you really think this is the best time to come out to her?"

He shuffles his feet against the blacktop. "There isn't going to be a better time, is there?"

She inhales again. Smoke curls from the corner of her mouth. "That's very selfish. Let her die in ignorance."

"Without really knowing me?"

"Mom knows what she needs to know."

It gets dark. Back in the kitchen, Julie turns off the overhead light. The only illumination comes from the range hood over the stove.

"It's been a long day." Her yawn is exaggerated. He knows it's a hint. "I should get some rest. I'm going to need a lot of strength over the next day or two."

"*We're* going to need strength," he corrects her, and she surprises him with a tight embrace.

"Yeah, little brother, *we*, not *me*." She tightens her hold on him and sighs into his ear. "This sounds horrible—I know it does—but I just want it to be over. For her. For me. For you."

Before she can leave the kitchen he asks, "Does Tom Melvin

still work at Gus's?"

The question seems to annoy her. "You've been home for less than two hours, our mother is dying upstairs and now you want to organize a reunion with your high school buddies?"

"I'd just like to see him. To say hi." This much is true enough. Also true, but unsaid, is that he has more unfinished business.

She frowns but hands him a key to the side door. "Don't stay out too late. I'm tired of doing this alone."

Gus's service station is across the street from the Sonic on Fast Food Alley. It's known locally for quick, honest auto work and cheap cigarettes and beer.

Tom Melvin manages the mini-mart, and Carver sees him through the window when he pulls the rental car into a space next to the air hose. He wonders if Tom will recognize him when he gets out of the car. He's a different Carver DeMaris—fancier clothes and fancier hair than the young man who left Patience all those years ago—but he supposes the façade won't be hard to see through.

The door chimes when Carver enters the mini-mart. For a few moments he glances around, transfixed by the overlit rows of Doritos, Slim Jims and stacked twelve-packs of Bud Light.

Then he turns, faces Tom and smiles. "Long time, no see."

Tom's expression is distant, his eye contact tentative. Carver thinks maybe he *doesn't* recognize him, until Tom finally speaks.

"How you doin', Carver?"

"Hanging in there, I guess."

Carver hasn't seen him in years, but Tom hasn't changed. Dark hair cropped short, broad shoulders, tight waist. He looks good. Better than ever.

Tom nods. "Heard about your mom. Sorry."

At the reference to his mother, Carver's face flushes and he looks away, down an aisle toward a stacked tower of Pringles canisters. "Yeah, it's pretty bad. Julie says she probably has a couple of days at the most."

"Damn, man, that's rough." During the long pause that follows, Tom starts restacking a pyramid of snack cakes next to the register. He's still stacking when he finds his voice again. "Too young. What, sixty?"

"Sixty-three. Yeah, too young."

"Well...sorry."

Long seconds pass. Carver stares at Pringles canisters. Tom restacks snack cakes.

Finally, Tom clears his throat. "So can I get you anything?"

Carver looks at him for the first time since he discovered the Pringles Tower. "I'm good."

"Slim Jim?"

"Nah."

"Hot dog that's been on the grill since last April?"

Carver laughs. "No, thanks."

Tom pauses. "So if you don't want anything, what brings you out tonight?"

There's an uncharacteristic quaver in Carver's voice. "I came to see you."

Tom's eyes narrow. It makes him even harder to read. "Well, you found me."

Carver knows he can't leave it at that. "I've been thinking a lot about the old days. High school." He pauses, not sure he can finish the thought. But he does. "I wish things had turned out differently. I wish I'd handled things better."

This is something they've never really talked about, and it sends Tom into another long silence before he speaks again.

"We were kids," he says generously. His cheeks dimple when

he smiles. "It happens. And, you know, the thing with your mother."

"Yeah. That." Carver can't look Tom in the eyes, so he looks at the floor.

"Things turned out okay for you, so no regrets. You're living in New York now, right?" Carver nods at the floor. "And it looks like you're doing well in—whatever you do."

Carver looks up. "Real estate."

"Cool." Tom's smile falters. Left unsaid is that he earns his paycheck managing a mini-mart.

"I came out." The shift in Carver's voice is abrupt. "When I moved to New York I didn't want to live a lie anymore."

Now Tom's smile has vanished altogether. "Are you out to your mother?"

"No. But my sister knows."

"Close enough, I guess."

"And, uh, you? Are you seeing anyone?"

Tom shakes his head. "Slim pickings here in Patience, Colorado. Sometimes I get away to Denver, but nothing serious."

"So..." says Carver.

"So..." echoes Tom.

Carver's discomfort returns. He knows why he came here, but he's not sure what he hopes to accomplish.

"I guess I'd better get back," he says finally.

Tom extends his hand. "Good seeing you again, Carver. And I know your mother had a problem with me, but I'm really sorry. I'll say a prayer."

As Carver is leaving, he looks back. They catch each other stealing one final glance.

They chuckle, but it's an awkward moment.

* * *

Carver climbs the stairs to his mother's bedroom. An old song is playing softly on Julie's iPad.

"Mom. It's me. It's Ben. I'm here." His real name sounds foreign to him. They started calling him Carver in middle school, after some neighborhood kids discovered his hobby of soap carving. The hobby lasted two weeks; the nickname stuck.

His mother breathes shallowly but doesn't open her eyes.

Julie's iPad, propped on the nightstand, repeats the song.

"So, Jules, what's the deal with the song you're torturing Mom with?" Carver asks his sister in the morning.

Julie's eyes are puffy and red rimmed. She sets her empty coffee cup in the sink and rinses it. "You mean 'Goody, Goody?' I know. But it's the only thing she'll listen to."

"Nonstop?"

Julie picks up the ceramic cup and drops it. It lands with a loud thump that shuts him up.

"Listen, Carver, I've been handling this situation alone for months. A visiting nurse every now and then, but mostly it's just me. I know what she wants, and she wants 'Goody, Goody.' So let her listen to whatever she wants to fuckin' listen to."

He's too shocked to put up a fight. "I just thought maybe a little variety..."

She shakes her head. Makes it clear that, to her, he's just another visiting nurse who knows nothing. "For weeks, every time I'm within twenty feet of her room, I have to hear that damn song. Over and over and over again. But you know what? She's the one who's dying, so she gets to hear it." Julie does the coffee-cup-drop thing again. The unspoken sibling communication they share tells him she means business and her little brother had better watch his ass.

She grabs a cigarette from the pack and motions to him. He's afraid not to follow.

"Here's the deal." She waves the cigarette for emphasis. "We're talking dementia, not just cancer. Dr. Hamilton thinks it's because of the drugs, but I don't know about that. She's been forgetful and confused for a while. If 'Goody, Goody' helps keep her grounded, I don't give a damn."

Carver tries to recover. "Sorry, Jules, I didn't realize."

"That's because *you're* never around. Lucky me! I'm the one who only moved to Denver, so I'm always a few hours away. Ninety minutes if I ride the gas pedal."

He looks past her to the marigolds in the backyard. "How long has she been, uh…?"

Julie shrugs. "A couple of years. It wasn't bad at first, but after the diagnosis she really started slipping."

"Sorry." He knows he sounds weak.

Julie doesn't seem to hear him. She takes a drag from her cigarette, blows the smoke away from the house, closes her eyes tightly and says, "It always has to be 'Goody-fuckin'-Goody.'"

And then she starts crying. Crying and smoking. In the driveway of a house that'll soon be one more stop on the Patience Death-and-Desertion Vacancy Tour.

"I'm sorry," she says, rallying. "I'm just so tired."

Carver sort of hugs her. Julie blows smoke away from his face and sort of hugs him back.

Later, when she's more or less back in control, she says, "Who'd ever think our god-fearing mother would get hooked on a recording by a guy who died of a heroin overdose fifty years ago?"

"What's that?" he asks.

"She'll only listen to one version of 'Goody, Goody.' The one by Frankie Lymon. Put another version on and she freaks."

Carter appreciates the irony. "He died from an OD?"

"Back in the Sixties. Only twenty-five years old."

"A year younger than I am now," Carver says.

She points at him. "That song might be the DeMaris Family Curse."

Later he takes a butter knife from the utensil drawer and uses it to pry up a floorboard in his bedroom. He's done this before, but this time, like that last drive into Patience past the high school and post office and Cookley Park and Fast Food Alley, is notable. This will be the Last Pry.

The floorboard finally pops up. The manila folder is still there, coated with dust.

He brushes off the folder and opens it to the top sheet of paper. It's a poem. A love poem. Flushed with embarrassment, he stops reading after two lines and tucks the folder full of bad poetry and unmailed letters into his suitcase.

There's a gentle rap on his bedroom door. He shoves the folder deeper into his suitcase before answering.

"It's almost time." Julie's voice is very professional. Clinical, as if she'd turned off some emotional switch. "If you have anything to tell her, you'd better tell her now."

"Thanks."

Still professional, she adds, "I can't stop you from saying anything you feel compelled to say, but remember who this is about."

He nods his understanding, and then walks down the hall and opens the door to his mother's room. Frankie Lymon sings 'Goody, Goody' from the iPad.

"Mom?"

The old woman's eyes open slightly.

"There's something I need to tell you." He senses his sister's presence in the doorway. Watching him. Wanting to know if he's going to say it.

Carver looks at his mother's gray face. She's sixty-three years old and looks forty years older.

"Mom, I'm—" He glances over his shoulder at Julie. She frowns.

He tries to swallow, but his throat is too dry.

"Mom," he starts again, but his will is broken. "Mom, I love you. And I'll see you again in heaven."

His sister sits next to him on the three wooden steps from the driveway to the kitchen door, no doubt happy he finally made a decision she agrees with.

Dr. Hamilton arrives in a car driven by his comparatively youthful seventy-year-old assistant and goes directly to their mother's bedroom.

Within the hour, Lois Howe DeMaris is dead.

After her body has been removed and they're alone, Julie lights another cigarette. He wouldn't think of stopping her. She deserves it.

"You know what?" She taps the fragment of an ash on the asphalt. "We're orphans."

A sad smile creeps across Carver's face. "Goody, Goody."

"Yeah." She leans back. "Goody, Goody." Julie looks at the cigarette in her hand. "The first thing I'm going to do after I'm done with this drama is delete that fucking song from my iPad."

Carver looks out at the small garden and wonders who will now tend the marigolds. A life has ended, but he'd rather focus on the imminent demise of the pretty things left behind.

* * *

Carver DeMaris is wearing a black pin-striped suit, tailored to a perfect fit on his lean body. His tie is a vivid yellowish orange. That morning he'd wondered if he shouldn't opt for more somber neckwear before deciding against it. He'll claim the tie honors his mother's beloved marigolds if anyone questions its appropriateness. The truth is that he just likes the tie, so he's going to wear it.

He's still in the black suit and marigold tie when he drives to Gus's a few hours after burying his mother.

As Carver checks his reflection in the car window, he sees Tom watching him from inside the mini-mart. He pockets his sunglasses and walks to the front door. The chime announces his arrival.

Carver manages a smile. Tom doesn't. This strikes Carver as strange, since he's the one who's come from his mother's funeral and Tom has only been selling gallons of unleaded and cases of Coors.

"You didn't think I'd come back, did you?"

"Always good to see you." Tom picks up a plastic donation jar for the Lions Club and holds it with one hand while dusting the surface with the palm of the other. Without looking up, he asks, "Are you okay?"

Carver shrugs. "Okay enough. All things considered."

"Good. Be strong, man."

"I will." Carver's smile fades. "It was a nice service, except the minister kept getting her name wrong."

Tom snorts and sets the Lions Club jar back on the counter. "You're kidding."

"Wish I was. I think the church meant more to her than she meant to the church."

"Yeah, well..." Tom's eyes wander to anything that isn't

Carver. He stammers before finally managing to get some words out. "Can I help you with anything?"

Carver stares at Tom for a long time, trying to read him. Every time he thinks he sees Tom from high school inside Tom the adult—strong, handsome, gentle Tom, the teenager he ran away from—the image shifts and he's looking at a stranger. He knows he brought this on himself. He's not happy about that.

"Can I help you with anything?" Tom asks again. It's an open-ended question and Carver has one answer he won't verbalize.

"I'm good," he finally says. "I just wanted to see you again before I head back to New York."

Tom's smile is sad, but it's a smile. "Take care of yourself."

Carver walks out the door. The chime makes more noise than his departing footsteps. When he backs the rental car out of its parking spot, he sees Tom standing in the window. Still watching.

It's two A.M. and Carver can't sleep. Every time his head hits the pillow, his mind races. To calm himself, he sneaks back to the kitchen, where a large bottle of merlot sits on the linoleum countertop. He'd bought it earlier, figuring he might need it. He does.

He refills his glass and considers toasting his dead mother before remembering she'd die all over again if she knew he'd brought alcohol into her home.

The clock ticks off another minute. Crucified Jesus watches him from the wall.

Carver decides to toast Jesus. At least *he* appreciated wine.

He has an inspiration. It has more to do with merlot than Jesus, but he'll give him the credit.

When Carver wakes up, it's only minutes before it's not

morning anymore. He immediately remembers and just as immediately regrets what he did in the middle of the night, but regrets won't do him any good at this point.

He pulls on a T-shirt and cargo shorts. Stubs a toe against the floorboard that never quite fit back into place after he'd pried it up with the butter knife. Grasps the injured toe. Curses. Even though she's dead and buried, he senses his mother's disapproval.

In the kitchen, the empty wine bottle taunts his foolishness. A marigold is stuck in the stem, which rattles him until he realizes Julie must have posed the flower.

She's sitting on the steps off the kitchen, smoking.

"You smoke too much."

"You drink too much. Or so says the huge empty bottle on the kitchen counter." She blows smoke directly at his face. "Don't even *try* to judge me."

They stare at the marigolds and don't speak.

Later Carver sits at the kitchen table and taps on the laptop keyboard. When his mother was alive they almost never used the living room or dining room, and now that she's dead, he and Julie continue the family tradition of avoiding half the house. They only use the kitchen and their bedrooms.

Julie has relaxed. She'd made it clear she wasn't in the mood to be judged, but that storm has passed.

She looks over her brother's shoulder. The screen displays the mock-up of a fuselage.

"Whatcha doing?"

Carver stares ahead at the screen. "Checking in for my flight tonight."

He finishes and closes the laptop, then turns toward her. "I hate that my life was a secret from Mom."

She considers that. "She wouldn't have approved. She wouldn't understand."

"Maybe not. But no more secrets, okay?"

She can read him, and he can read her. That's their sibling connection. He knows she senses more drama is coming, despite her many protestations over previous days.

Julie groans. Flips her hair. Closes her eyes. Reopens them. "I think I need another cigarette."

This time Julie lights up in the kitchen. No more mother, no more rules.

Carver clears his throat. "I want to be with Tom."

"Tom?" She's lost until it clicks. "Tom *Melvin*?" He nods. "Are you telling me Tom's gay?" Clearly she'd never considered the possibility. Just as clearly, she's seldom thought of Tom in *any* context.

Carver doesn't directly answer her. "I should have done this a long time ago. I'm just feeling bolder right now."

"Would you be this bold if Mom was still alive?"

"Probably not. Patience is both a virtue and a *very* small town." He trails off, wondering how committed he is to baring his secret. Committed enough, he decides. "There's something you don't know."

Julie taps ashes into the sink. "Do I *want* to know?"

He thinks she probably doesn't, but that won't stop him. No more secrets, after all. "Back in high school, Tom and I, we—we sort of had a thing."

"Seriously?" She seems legitimately shocked to hear her little brother wasn't a virginal teenager. "You mean you two—?"

He nods. "For a few months."

She taps ashes into the sink again. "Well, damn, you're full of surprises today. So what happened?"

"I couldn't handle it. I just—" Words fail him and he takes

a deep breath to collect his thoughts. "I was afraid that people would find out I was gay, and I couldn't let that happen. So I blamed it on Mom. Told Tom that she figured things out and said we couldn't be friends anymore."

She shakes her head disapprovingly. "You used Mom as an excuse?"

He knows he was wrong but can't help feeling defensive. "She *wouldn't* have approved, Jules."

Julie stubs out the cigarette next to the drain and leaves the butt in the basin. Judgment is heavy in her voice. "True, but she *didn't* know. Why didn't you just tell Tom the truth?"

Carver's feeling of shame swells. "Look, I'm not nominating myself as a profile in courage. I was flawed. Still am. But now I want to make things right. And I want to be with him again."

Her voice assumes the tone of the Wise Older Sibling. "Then you'll have to tell him the truth."

"I already did."

"When?"

More shame. Carver wonders if it's limitless. "Back in high school, I wrote him a letter. Told him everything."

She looks relieved. "Okay, so he knows about your lie. That makes this a *little* better."

He wants to end the conversation but knows if it stops, there will always be a secret between them. "The thing is, I never mailed the letter."

"I'm not sure I follow..."

"I slipped it under the door of the mini-mart last night."

Julie's jaw drops. "Oh, shit."

He now knows the depths of shame are limitless.

Carver DeMaris guides his rental car across the abandoned railroad tracks and past the peeling sign reading "Leaving Patience:

It's A Virtue."

Saying good-bye to Julie was difficult. In a sense, despite their sometimes difficult relationship, she's always been the love of his life. Not, of course, in the same sense as Tom.

He hopes Tom will forgive him. He hopes Tom will want to rekindle the relationship abandoned so long ago when Carver was a frightened teenager.

He's also prepared for rejection, which he knows is a much more likely outcome.

Carver turns the key in the ignition and the engine dies. He sits behind the wheel for a moment and takes a few deep breaths. Then he looks out the windshield at the mini-mart and gathers his courage.

Tom barely looks at him when he walks through the door.

Carver swallows hard. "You're angry."

Tom takes his time answering. Finally, he says, "Yes." Then he says, "No."

Carver is confused. "Yes *and* no?" He wishes Tom's emotions were clearer. At least he'd know—*something*. "Tom? Look, I'm sorry."

Tom glares at Carver, who begins to wish Tom's emotions were less clear again. "I'm pissed that you blamed your mother, and I'm pissed it took you ten years to tell me the truth. So yes, I'm angry."

Carver tries to speak. Tom holds out a hand to silence him.

"I'm also pissed at myself for wasting my life in Patience. Not moving to Denver or someplace else where I could have a real life." He sighs. The harshness in his voice loses its edge. "So I guess I've got a lot of anger to spread around."

"It's not too late," says Carver. "Come to New York with me."

"Is *that* why you're here?" Tom asks. Carver smiles hopefully. "I can't see that happening."

It's hard to argue, but Carver tries. "It's never too late to start a new life."

"A new life." Tom's tone is dismissive. "Who gets a new life?"

Carver's voice is tiny. "I did."

Tom finally manages a smile. "I guess you did. And that's why I can't be angry with you, no matter how much I'd like to be. You found some courage and made something of yourself. You came out. Maybe not to your mother, but you did it. And you're finally being honest with me. It took you ten years, but you did it. Me, I'm just stuck. Stuck in a small town in the middle of nowhere. Each day like every other day."

Carver pleads, "Leave. I'll—look, I'll even buy your ticket." When Tom doesn't respond, he adds, "I'd like to start over again. Not as a scared kid, but as an adult."

Maybe Tom appreciates Carver's persistence, but it's clear he isn't going to jump into the rental car, and he isn't going to fly away with Carver.

When Carver walked into the mini-mart, he'd thought there were two possible outcomes: Tom would fall back into his arms, or Tom would reject him.

While he preferred the first possibility to the second, either would give Carver closure.

"I'm not ready to make a decision," Tom said. "I understand why you did what you did ten years ago, but I need to think about things."

His decision is a big Maybe. Carver hadn't counted on a third option. But in that option, he finds hope.

Carver thinks he understands why Tom needs to protect

himself. And they both understand that, individually or as a couple, they need to move forward.

The conversation ended with a lingering kiss. There was still passion after all those years.

That's good enough for Carver.

He knows a song about a broken relationship sung by a man who overdosed at twenty-five doesn't fit the situation, but he can't help singing "Goody, Goody" as his car speeds west toward Denver.

SPILL YOUR TROUBLES ON ME, LOVE

Georgina Li

Ethan grabbed the big gray hoodie from his locker in the train station, pulled it on over his black tank and hopped on the train. There was a guy crashed out across five or six seats at the far end of the car, but other than that it was empty. Ethan sat by the door, pulled his knees up close to his chest and wiped his mouth on his sleeve. It left a little smear of cherry lip balm on the fabric, but Ethan didn't much care. He was off for the next thirty-six hours, and Rosie's Bakery was only three stops away.

Rosie's had become a ritual from the first time Lucas brought him there and Mrs. Cammelli fussed over them and made Ethan blush. Ethan stopped there every Tuesday morning, and old Mrs. Cammelli spoiled him just like she did Lucas. There was something about it that felt right. Sometimes Ethan fantasized about giving up the life and working at Rosie's like Mrs. Cammelli, or maybe even working in the back like Mr. Cammelli, wearing an apron and singing to his pastry while he measured and kneaded and baked. It was crazy, and it was never going to happen, but Ethan liked the idea of it anyway. He couldn't turn tricks forever.

This morning he bought two buttery croissants and splurged on two chocolate ones, too, still warm from the big ovens in the back. Mrs. Cammelli fixed two large to-go cups of steaming hot tea, one for him and one for Lucas, sweetened with the thick condensed milk he loved without his even having to ask. Ethan walked the two blocks to their apartment humming to himself. The city was as quiet as it ever got, buses and street cleaners and someone's car alarm going off, boys like Ethan heading home after a long night, street vendors setting up.

Ethan's building was mostly dark still, the stairwell filthy, more rank than usual. He carefully made his way up to their floor, opened the door to the squat he shared with Lucas with one hand, tea and croissants balanced in the other.

Inside, Lucas was slumped against the wall, jeans around his thighs and his dick soft, vomit on his shirt. Ethan leaned back against the door for a minute, took in the sight. He set their breakfast down on the table, making room among the tangled strands of tiny lights Lucas had found the day before. Ethan closed his eyes for a minute, imagined the lights were hanging above their bed already just like they'd talked about, white and gold like so many stars, close enough to touch, and he and Lucas were sprawled out beneath them.

Ethan kicked off his shoes, scrubbed his fingers through his hair. It was long enough now that he could tuck it behind his ears, pale curls that reeked of spunk and sweat and dirty hands. He'd hack it off but he'd been earning heavy lately and he knew it was the hair. It made him look younger than he was, more vulnerable.

Lucas shifted on the floor and licked his lips, made a low sort of sound, slurry and almost like words. Ethan rubbed his hand over Lucas's shaved head, the soft buzz of bristles making his skin tingle, and Lucas blinked up at him, smiling. Ethan dropped down beside him for a while, leaning his head on Lucas's shoulder. One of his regulars had been in a shit mood tonight, couldn't get it up until Ethan was bloody, shaking.

Lucas touched Ethan's swollen lip carefully, the bruises on his throat. "Hey there, beautiful," Lucas said and pulled him a little closer.

Last week they'd dragged a mattress up the stairs, big enough for both of them and hardly stained at all. Lucas took their old one down to the alley, left a note on it: FREE TO A GOOD HOME. Ethan had added a smiley face to it when he headed out that afternoon and wasn't surprised at all to find the mattress gone when he came home.

Ethan looked at their bed, scratched at his belly, said, "Okay, fucker, time to get up. We both need showers," and Lucas burped and swallowed hard, reached out a hand when Ethan stood up again. Lucas's skin was hot and his palm was scraped to hell, but Ethan pulled him to his feet carefully and brushed a kiss across his cheek. Lucas grinned at him and held up his pants with his free hand.

Ethan watched him check his pocket for the money he kept hidden inside. Then his hand drifted to his dog tags—CRADY, LUCAS, M., 045265894, O NEG, CATHOLIC—which clinked together softly as he looked for his guitar case. It was a familiar ritual, and as usual, Lucas didn't breathe easy until he found his baby propped up by the door. "So," he said, "did I piss myself?"

Ethan laughed and shook his head. It was important to have priorities. "Not this time," he said, squinting to get a closer look at Lucas's hand. Dirt and blood, little bits of what looked like gravel. He'd have a fuck of a time playing for the next few days, but it didn't look too bad. Ethan turned Lucas's palm over and brought the thick knuckles to his lips. It was sweet, the way Lucas's cheeks flushed at that, bright pink splotches on his pale skin, but Ethan just shrugged, unembarrassed. "Looks like you puked, though."

"Might do that again in a minute," Lucas said. Ethan pointed toward the window by their bed.

Asking Lucas not to drink was like asking a trick not to be an asshole; it just wasn't going to happen. Ethan didn't even want it to. He liked Lucas the way he was. Besides, the tricks who pretended not to be assholes were always the worst in the end, and that was just a fact.

Ethan grabbed their good towel and the dish soap from the crate in the corner, found some clean clothes tucked underneath. Faded jeans and thick blue sweatpants, a couple of long-sleeved cotton tees. It made his heart beat hot thinking about Lucas down at the St. Francis shop without him, picking out things Ethan could wear only at home, touching everything, making sure it was soft.

Lucas pushed at the window, coughed until his whole body was shaking with it and spit into the alley below. He didn't puke, but he didn't sound good, either, and Ethan thought they should probably go to the clinic. Soon, Ethan promised himself, kicking a pair of flip-flops in Lucas's general direction. He gathered up the dirty dishes from around the room: three forks and four spoons, a bowl, a couple of mugs Lucas nicked from the truck stop Ethan worked only when he was desperate. Last time he got beat up pretty good, broken ribs and antibiotics he couldn't afford, and he'd lost his take for the night, too.

Man, that was a shitty week. Lucas had gone out in his place to make it up, but he wasn't Ethan, wasn't even the right type. Lucas earned in the subways mostly, black felt hat and his guitar thrumming in his hands, his voice rough and open, songs that made the city feel timeless, old and somehow new again, too. Ethan thought he sounded like a fallen angel when he was singing in the tunnels, especially when the trains were rolling through.

Lucas said he'd missed his guitar more than anyone when he was overseas, said he hadn't felt like he was home until he had an acoustic in his hands again. He'd stopped at a pawnshop as soon as he was stateside and picked his new baby right off the wall. He didn't talk about being over there much, though sometimes he had nightmares, or he'd say things like "racked out" or "squared away," and Ethan would grin and imagine him in uniform, sexy and sharp. Mostly it made Ethan sort of sad to think about Lucas serving his country and hiding who he was, made him wish they'd known each other then, too. Ethan would have written him letters, made sure he had something to miss for real.

Ethan heard the window close, the solid thunk of wood on wood, glass rattling in its casing. By the time Lucas slung his arm around Ethan's shoulders he was humming to himself, almost steady on his feet. Christ, he was gorgeous, his dark hair just growing in and his milky skin all scarred up. He was sweating booze and stale smoke, but his eyes were bright when he looked at Ethan, blue as the ocean, blue as the whole world.

"Look what I got today," Lucas said, digging a toothbrush still in its packaging from his pocket, and a tiny tube of toothpaste, too. "Someone dropped these in my case. Maybe it was a dentist? Or a joke." Lucas frowned for a second before he smiled again. "Who the fuck cares, right? It's as good as money."

"It's better, fuck." If they could afford it, Ethan would use a new toothbrush every day. Fuck, he'd use two. He had a thing about it, but Lucas didn't care, would kiss him right on the mouth no matter how many johns he'd been with that night, whether he'd brushed his teeth or not. He never shied away from Ethan, from the bruises, from the way he lived his life; never made him feel like he was dirty, used up. Lucas would run his fingers up and down the paths other men etched into his body, breathing whiskey songs into his skin, reshaping the streets with his hands, his lips, his tongue.

"Water's running next floor down," Lucas said, and Ethan smiled, happy they wouldn't have to go looking. Showers with Lucas were the best, the slip-slide of their soapy bodies, the way Lucas would press himself against Ethan, all big muscles and tender skin, and fuck him long and slow. Lucas would spread himself open sometimes, too, fingers scrabbling against the broken tiles, so close with Ethan's dick barely inside him; he'd moan and gasp and shoot his load, just from the feel of them together. God, he was amazing.

Afterward they'd stumble back upstairs all clean and lemon-scented. They'd eat their croissants and drink their tea sitting cross-legged in their new bed, the morning sun shining through the windows and their knees bumping together, ratty blankets piled high.

Ethan reached for the door then, ready to put the night behind him. He paused midway, his hand hovering over the table, bypassing the tangled lights and reaching for his tea instead. The paper cup was warm in his hand still, and the tea was delicious, strong and sweet. It was his favorite, and Lucas's favorite, too.

"Mrs. Cammelli make that for you?" Lucas asked, and Ethan nodded and licked his lips. And then, "Croissants, too?" He sounded so hopeful, his eyes darting over to the crinkled bakery bag, and Ethan nodded again, smiling. Lucas took a swig from his bottle and wrapped his arms around Ethan, kissed him real slow. "You're too good to me," Lucas said, but Ethan knew it wasn't true.

They were good to each other, and that's just the way it was. Even this, right now, Lucas's body against his, heavy and alive, his hand curled on Ethan's shoulder, his thumb rubbing along the curve of Ethan's throat. It was perfect.

"You want to hang the lights later?" Lucas asked, and Ethan smiled then, too. "Cool," Lucas said. He took a swig from his bottle and wrapped his arms around Ethan, kissed him some more, careful for Ethan's bruises. Lucas was always careful with him, but not too careful, not like Ethan was fragile or broken. The way Lucas touched him, the way he kissed, made Ethan feel like he was the only thing that mattered. It was intense. And it made Ethan's heart beat fast, made him press closer, made him want.

"Happy Tuesday," Lucas said, lips brushing against Ethan's as he spoke, shivery hot, making Ethan feel like stars inside, like light, bright and beautiful.

"Happy Tuesday," Ethan said back, laughing, and Lucas laughed, too, like an echo, only better. They were going to make it, Ethan thought, suddenly. They were totally going to make it. He'd never been more sure.

QUALITY TIME

Lewis DeSimone

We don't sleep together when Sarah's visiting. Victor's afraid she would be traumatized by the sight of her father in bed with another man. So every other Saturday morning, I make up the convertible sofa in the study and sprinkle a few of my things around the room to give it that lived-in feel. The bottom desk drawer is full of socks and underwear; shirts and pants are crushed together in the tiny closet, fighting for space with empty stereo boxes and the barbells neither of us ever has the energy to use. I keep a pile of books by the computer—without a warm body beside me at night, I often have to read for hours before I can fall asleep. An adult would never believe that anyone could survive in such cramped quarters for more than a weekend, but it's Sarah we're trying to fool. She's only five. While she sleeps in the guest room and her father sprawls across our king-size bed, I toss and turn, trying to avoid the bar that runs like a jagged spine beneath the thin mattress.

We've been living like this for six months now, since I moved into Victor's Beacon Hill apartment. "Please, Greg," he said back then, "it's only temporary. Once Sarah gets used to you, we can sleep in the same room and she won't think anything of it." Sarah got used to me pretty quickly, but here I am again, piling sofa cushions in a corner of the room so I'll have a place to sleep.

I've just pulled out the mattress when I hear them coming through the front door, Sarah's high-pitched rambling about the latest intrigue in preschool, every sentence ending with a plaintive "you know what?" to lead her to her next point. Victor calls my name over the continuous murmur.

"In here!" I snap a fitted sheet into the air. Black and white stripes, faded in the middle to gray, the sheets I used for years in what Victor still refers to as my "bachelor pad."

Victor's voice falls to a gentle, diplomatic tone. "Honey, why don't you go in your room for a minute and play? I'll have a surprise for you later."

His words, meant to calm her down, have backfired; Sarah's practically shrieking. "Surprise? What surprise?"

"You'll see," he says, "but you have to be good." Victor's patience with Sarah, his ability to bury the more demanding part of his nature in her presence, has a way of stopping me in my tracks. In a moment, Sarah's humming softly to herself, a tune she makes up as she goes along, and the guest room door closes behind her.

Victor appears in the doorway of the study. "Hi," he says, watching me tuck the sheet around the mattress. He's had the convertible since business school; the back is starting to leak its stuffing in spots. It's no wonder he didn't have to fight with Christina for this thing; she was content with the Danish stuff.

"Hi. How is she?"

"She's fine. I'm the one who's a complete wreck." He's

leaning against the doorjamb, one blue-jeaned leg crossed over the other, the toe of his Topsider pointing to the floor. He pulls nervously at his beard. "Where are the tickets?"

"I don't know," I say, stifling a grunt as I stretch to reach the other side of the bed.

"Well, where do you suppose they are?" His eyes are pleading behind his glasses.

I spread the blanket and let it land, parachute-like, over the mattress. "Try the nightstand."

He vanishes like a little boy given permission for the cookie jar, and I start on the hospital corners. I'm fluffing the pillows when I hear him knock on Sarah's door across the hall. "Sweetheart, it's time for your surprise!"

I join him in the hall in time for the door to fly open. Sarah's jumping around, long brown hair bouncing in curls on the shoulders of her sweater. "What, Daddy? What?"

He holds the tickets in a fan above her head. She stops jumping and peers up at them. "Yeah?"

"We're going to the ballet tonight, sweetheart. *The Nutcracker*."

The peals of delight begin all over again, followed by questions. I watch with my own sense of delight as Victor tries to explain the plot. Struggling over the Sugar Plum Fairy, he turns to me. "Greg's coming, too," he says and Sarah notices me as if for the first time.

"Greg! Greg! We're going to *The Nutcracker*!" She dances around me, steps she's learned in ballet class, and leads us both into the living room, where she starts spinning in awkward circles. She's clearly too inexperienced for a pirouette, and I find myself standing guard over the furniture.

Beside me, Victor's smiling broadly, his anxiety washed away by his daughter's joy. This, I think, is what I love most about these weekends. With Sarah, Victor relaxes. With Sarah, he can be completely himself.

Sarah's excitement about the ballet carries her through the day. It's all she can talk about over lunch, though Victor's loaded her plate with the dreaded carrots she threw a tantrum over the last time. She squirms atop the Yellow Pages, a blizzard of energy.

From the beginning, Sarah has seemed to me more her mother's child than Victor's. Perhaps because she's a girl or because, like Christina, she entered my life as an interloper of sorts—an outsider in the sheltered male enclave. She has Christina's liveliness and curiosity—a willingness to ask questions of everyone and everything at any time—which particularly upsets Victor's characteristic reserve. When he introduced us in June, the weekend after I moved in, Sarah scowled at me for a long moment, her nose twitching as Victor's does when he's angry. "Is he going to be here all weekend?" she snarled, still staring. "Greg lives here now, Sarah," Victor said, causing her to spin around in shock. But by dinnertime, she'd become distracted by the truckload of new toys her father had bought to appease her (Victor's nothing if not prepared) and insisted on sitting beside me—as if I, too, were one of her new playthings.

We take a walk after lunch to the Public Garden. It's a surprisingly warm day for early December, but Victor still wraps a wool coat around Sarah. By the time we cross Beacon Street, beads of sweat are forming on her forehead. Looking askance at her father, she unbuttons the coat and puffs out a gentle sigh of relief.

In the park, she reaches her free hand toward mine, the other already clasped in Victor's. Together, we stroll along the winding path, Sarah swinging in the air as we lift her over puddles. She's unimpressed with the standard kiddie attraction, McCloskey's ducklings, not even deigning to leapfrog the bronze figures with the other children. Instead, she pulls us toward the lake, frozen now, crowded with circling ice skaters. We stop on the bridge, Sarah peering through the pale blue grate to watch. Beneath us, a young couple glides along the ice, hand in hand, the woman's light hair escaping from her hat in single strands. The man releases her for a spin and promptly plummets onto the ice. She helps him up, and they both laugh. As they hold hands once more and continue together, their movements seem all the more elegant, flecks of ice flying up in clouds behind their skates.

I haven't been to the ballet in years, not that I've missed it. Somehow I've never had a problem suspending disbelief in the opera house when an overweight diva coughs her way through an improbable case of TB, but the sight of a line of tutued anorexics tittering across the stage has been known to put me into hysterics. Fortunately *The Nutcracker* has enough semblance of a plot to keep me distracted.

Sarah, on the other hand, is enthralled. She's still wide-awake at intermission, eyes glowing from the spectacle. The three of us go out to the mezzanine and look down at the lobby, where the thirsty and overdressed crowd around the bar.

"What do you think so far, angel?" Victor asks, hoisting Sarah onto the railing. He sets her sideways, against a pillar, so she can gaze comfortably at the buzzing crowd, and clutches her tightly around the middle.

"Can I be in it someday, Daddy?"

"Sure you can. If you want to."

She smiles brightly, tiny gaps showing between her teeth. A thick tress of her hair is tied in back with a white ribbon, leaving two long chestnut curls to frame her face. Her wide eyes scan the lobby, intrigued by everything they see. Victor, close behind, looks down at her head, indifferent to everything else. Sarah is the only thing that matters.

Leaning against the next pillar, I turn in the other direction, toward the crowd that meanders through the mezzanine. A familiar voice pierces through and all at once Harlan is coming toward me. He has an entourage—Bill, Robert and Edward bringing up the rear, leaning in for whispers behind his back. Edward looks well, almost filling out his gray jacket. His hair is thicker than the last time I saw him; I wonder if it will ever fully grow back.

I step away from the rail to meet them. "Hey," Harlan calls, "what are you doing here? I thought you hated this stuff."

"Hi, guys." I try to get them all in one sweeping glance. "We have Sarah for the weekend," I explain. "She loves the ballet."

Bill pulls away and moves toward the rail. "So this is the famous Sarah, eh?" He spreads his legs out to bring his lanky frame down to her level.

"Sarah," Victor says, "say hi to my friend Bill."

Sarah, as usual, is more curious than friendly. She smiles and lets out a garbled hello before falling into a long-held stare at Bill's tie, studying it like a Technicolor Rorschach blot.

"She's adorable," Robert says, sidling up beside me for a better view. He's grown a mustache since I last saw him. He looks older.

"You must be so proud, dear," Harlan adds. "The stretch marks don't even show."

I ignore him and turn my attention to Robert and Edward. "How are you enjoying the ballet?"

"It's wonderful," Edward says. His voice is softer, as if his weight loss has given it less room to reverberate in his chest. "I haven't seen this one in ages; I'd forgotten how much I love it."

Robert places an arm lightly against Edward's back; I can't tell whether the support is emotional or physical. "I'm not much of an aficionado," he says, "but Edward's teaching me the ropes. I'll probably start to appreciate it in a decade or so."

Edward is the first to laugh. It gives the rest of us permission.

"Let me say hello to Victor," Harlan says, moving swiftly past me. Nothing pleases Harlan more than putting Victor on the spot. I fall in behind, for protection.

"You're awfully big for five," Bill is saying, squinting at Sarah. His natural affinity for children has already completely won her over.

"What's shaking, Victor?" Harlan asks, slipping in beside him.

"Not much. And you?" Victor's arms seem just an inch tighter around Sarah's belly. Perhaps it's simply that she's leaned forward to continue her discussion with Bill. She whispers to him, eyes set in a serious expression, as if she's dispensing state secrets.

"Oh," Harlan coos, arms dramatically akimbo, "you know me. I'll shake it anywhere it gets a reaction." He winks back at me, certain he's scored a point.

Victor arches his neck to see over Harlan's shoulder. "Hi, Robert," he says, smiling at last. "How are you?" Harlan takes the hint and moves out of the way. Bill, still talking to Sarah, straightens up to stand beside her father.

Victor's expression changes suddenly as Robert and Edward come up together to greet him. Victor hasn't seen Edward in months, not even in the hospital. Hospitals are depressing, he said then, during the pneumocystis; he didn't know how to behave around sick people. I tried to tell him that you treat them the same way you should treat everyone else. The problem isn't that we generally patronize the sick, but that we're unkind to the healthy.

"She's really beautiful, Victor," Edward says. "Such lovely hair. It's Sarah, isn't it? Hi, Sarah." Edward reaches a bony hand forward to stroke Sarah's curls.

Victor flinches, abruptly clutching Sarah against him. She twists around and tries to pry his fingers away. I see then that his eyes are frozen wide—just for a second. He catches himself, and loosening his grip on Sarah, turns a sudden, embarrassed smile toward Edward, but it's too late. Edward's hand already hangs by his side. He, too, is smiling, both of them pretending that nothing has happened.

The lobby lights flicker, summoning us back to the auditorium. Victor lifts Sarah off the railing and holds her hand. Her fingers are lost in his, only the edge of her thumb showing. "Time to visit the Sugar Plum Fairy," he says.

I let Victor and Sarah go ahead and stay behind to say goodbye to the others. Edward's glancing down at the lobby, feigning indifference. I resist the urge to hug him, to apologize on Victor's behalf.

At least I can always count on Harlan. "Well, back to the kiddie show," he says, rolling his eyes. "I don't know why I let you people talk me into these things. It's like 'Pee-wee's Playhouse' on Valium."

Edward laughs, pats him on the back. "We'll teach you yet," he says.

I leave them at the stairs to the balcony, amid promises of phone calls and dinner dates. By the time I get back to my seat, the lights are dim, Sarah and Victor staring at the still-lowered curtain. The second act, I recall, is even more boring than the first—no plot this time, just acrobatics. I settle back and turn my eyes to the ceiling, concentrating on the repeated patterns of the music.

Victor tucks Sarah in and comes, yawning, into the living room. "She's exhausted," he says. "She'll sleep like a log."

"It *is* way past her bedtime." I'm sitting in the armchair, skimming through *Newsweek*. The *Advocate* has been removed to the study for the weekend.

"Did you have a good time tonight?" He's hovering in the center of the room, stretching his arms luxuriously above his head.

"Truth?" I ask.

He looks startled. "Of course."

"Right. I forgot. You always want the truth." I toss the magazine onto the coffee table.

He tries to laugh it off. "Maybe I should have asked for a white lie."

"Do you have any idea how rude you were to my friends tonight?"

"Apparently not." He drapes his jacket over the couch. "But if we're going to fight, maybe we should do it in another room, so we don't wake Sarah." He walks past me and through the swinging door into the kitchen.

He's standing by the refrigerator when I enter, holding the door open with his back as he pours club soda into a glass. "Look," he says, "if this is about Edward, I feel terrible. I just had a moment of panic." He shuts the refrigerator door and leans against the counter, sipping his soda. "I know there's no danger. I'm not that stupid. I just—"

"What?"

"If you had a child, you'd understand. It's not rational. It's instinct. You want to protect your child from everything, and sometimes that makes you do stupid things."

"I get it." And suddenly I feel like the jealous stepmother. Suddenly I *am* the jealous stepmother. "But you can't protect her from everything," I tell him. "And there are things she doesn't even need to be protected from."

"What do you mean?" He's tapping a finger nervously against the countertop—an outlet for repressed energy. Victor hates arguments. "Oh god," he says with a sigh. "Harlan?"

"He's my best friend, Victor, and you treat him like he isn't even there."

His look of exasperation takes the air out of the room. "I don't think Harlan is a particularly good influence on five-year-olds." He's whispering, which makes the words come out in a kind of hiss.

"I hardly think Sarah has any idea what he's talking about."

"That's not the point. All that sexual innuendo. Everything is sexual innuendo with Harlan. He has no life except between his legs."

"So it's not as much about protecting Sarah as it is about protecting your sensibilities?" The plant above the sink is drooping. I check the soil, which comes up dry on my finger. "There's a lot more to Harlan than you realize," I tell him.

"Harlan wears his sexual preference like a sandwich board."

"That's a problem? Letting the world know you're gay?" I place the plant beneath the faucet and let the water run in a thin stream.

"Is it necessary?"

I twist the faucet handle sharply to OFF. "In this world, yes, it is. Would you prefer he just slam the closet door and only come out at night, when all the kids have been put safely to bed?"

He drains his glass and pulls open the dishwasher to place

it in the rack. "Look, Greg, this isn't getting us anywhere. Let's just go to bed."

"Where?"

"Oh, is that what you're getting at?"

"Would it be so awful if Sarah knew the truth about her father? Would it be so terrible to raise a child with the knowledge that it's okay to be different? That gay doesn't mean perverse, that it's nothing to be ashamed of?"

"Why should I have to raise my daughter according to your political expectations? She's a child, not a social movement."

My heart is pounding. I give it a moment to rest. "You say I don't know anything about raising children. Well, I do know about *being* one. I know what I got from my own father, Victor. The look of disgust on his face when gay pride marches turned up on the news, the jokes he made about 'fags' and 'lesbos.' Those remarks turned me into a self-hater and my brothers into bigots."

"What does that have to do with Sarah?"

"How can she be proud of you if you're ashamed?"

"I'm not ashamed. I just don't define myself by who I sleep with."

"Who you sleep with? That's what it's all about—who you fuck?"

"Greg." He's gritting his teeth.

"No, Victor. Don't bother. If sex is the only thing that makes you gay, then you have nothing to worry about. You're welcome to be as hetero as you want." I push the door open. When I'm halfway across the living room, its squeaking stops abruptly in mid-swing.

We'd been dating for a month before Victor told me about Sarah, or the fact that he'd only recently left his wife. As he related, over a long dinner in a North End trattoria, the details of his path out of the closet—the slowly dawning awareness that something wasn't right, the secret pick-ups on business trips, the guilt when he turned away from Christina in bed and she thought it was her fault—I could reconcile none of it with the image I'd already constructed of him. I'd been drawn to Victor by his self-assurance, his masculine matter-of-factness. From the start, Victor represented pragmatism to me, rationality, fearlessness. Everything I was missing, he would supply.

And there he was, suddenly just a man, just as fragile as anyone else. He was no longer my ideal, my knight in shining armor. And that was the moment—I remember it still, his dark eyes in the candlelight—when I fell in love.

"Are you horrified?" he asked, his baritone voice suddenly so small, barely reaching me over the din of the restaurant.

"By what?" I said, smiling. I wanted to reach a hand across the table and caress his cheek, feel the heft of his beard on my palm. But already I knew his discomfort with public affection. After years of opening my own heart too quickly, too wide, I respected his restraint, his reticence. Victor taught me to slow down.

"I'm not like you," he said. "You're so present."

"Me?" I replied with a laugh. "You have no idea of the depths of my insecurity."

"That's just it," he said. "You're *aware*. You think about what you're feeling. You can even put it into words. I can't imagine that. I envy that."

"Then I guess I'll just have to teach you," I said.

He smiled, lines crinkling around his eyes. "I'd like that." And beneath the table, his knee pressed against mine, warm and strong.

Alone in the study now, I can't manage to read more than

a page before my eyes begin to flutter. Sleep is my escape from the world, my drug of choice. It used to be booze. This is an improvement.

And before I know it, I'm onstage, paralyzed in the bustle of dancers jumping and pirouetting around me. I've forgotten the choreography. Fear rises in my throat as the Nutcracker dances aside, clearing the way for my solo.

My breath catches, and suddenly the dream breaks apart. A floorboard creaks somewhere in the darkness. I'm about to roll over when a weight settles beside me. Victor's smell—bitter musk cut with something vaguely citrus—wafts toward me. Often, when I linger in bed after he's left early for work, I bury my nose in his pillow to recapture that scent.

He drapes an arm over me and draws himself closer, until my back is resting against the thick fur of his chest. He drops his head upon my shoulder and breathes deeply, his torso expanding behind me. His legs scissor into mine, heavy thighs squeezing me.

Then he rolls me over onto my back and anchors himself above me. His face is a silhouette hovering. He's looking at me—just looking, as if there's anything to see in the dark. He kisses me—one gentle kiss, then another—and a hand runs down my neck to my chest to my belly to my inner thigh. He caresses me, and we kiss again—longer this time, deeper.

We don't say a word. To avoid waking Sarah, perhaps, but mostly because we don't need to. I make my living with words, but Victor has taught me the poetry of silence.

Victor's usually the light sleeper—up with the sun. I'm the one who needs buzzing alarms to drag me out of bed. But the window in the study is small and betrays only the slightest hint of morning. I peer at the clock. It's already past seven.

His arm is a warm, dead weight on my back, but my shifting pulls him awake. He sighs, kisses the nape of my neck.

"It's late," I tell him. "Sarah will be up any minute." Another thing I learned a few months ago: how impossible it is to sleep in with a five-year-old in the house.

"She wants pancakes," he says.

"How do you know that?" I ask with a laugh.

He snuggles closer. "She told me last night. She wants pancakes."

"Okay, then you'd better start the batter." I kick him playfully.

"Five more minutes," he pleads.

"She'll be looking for you."

I feel the words on my skin more than I hear them. "It's okay."

I arch my back. "No, Victor, she shouldn't just stumble upon us. You should tell her first."

Words again.

"You're right." Slowly he pulls away, leaving a draft in his wake. I roll over, my back now on his side of the bed.

He's standing, pulling on his robe, closing it tight over his chest. "Good morning," he says with a smile. He leans down and kisses me.

I lie there for a while, listening to the sounds of breakfast. A few minutes later, I hear Sarah scuffle into the kitchen, their murmuring voices.

It's the smell of coffee that pulls me out of bed at last—that and a desperate need to pee. I dash into the bathroom. Sarah's singing softly in the kitchen. Behind the closed door, it sounds oddly like Madonna, but the words are her own: *Papa don't peach, I'm in double dip.*

By the time I'm presentable, they've finished their pancakes and moved to the living room, Victor ensconced on the couch, the newspaper in piles around him, and Sarah at his feet, working on a coloring book. They're planning a trip to the Children's Museum, Victor tells me, and perhaps the Tea Party Ship along the way. "Interested?" he asks, peering over the editorial section.

"Actually, I thought I'd just spend the day catching up on some work." I brought a manuscript home from the office on Friday, something from the slush pile that looked vaguely interesting; alone, I might be able to make a dent in it.

"Oh, Greg, come with us!" Sarah cries, looking up from her book. The crayons are spread before her on the carpet, spilling from the box, revealing their eccentric names. She's colored the Dalmatians maize-yellow, their spots periwinkle-blue.

"Sorry, sweetie, I can't today." I head for the kitchen to pour myself a thick dose of caffeine.

I catch Victor's eye on the way out of the room. His head tilted to one side, he seems to be pleading with me, too. Sarah isn't the only one who wants my company.

"Sorry," I say again, to them both now. "I have a deadline tomorrow. You'll have to try to have fun without me."

I'm pouring my second mug of coffee when Victor sidles quietly into the kitchen. He kisses the crown of my head.

Once Sarah has brushed her teeth and dressed (no simple task), they're out the door, and the place is all mine. Settled in my armchair, I cradle the heavy manuscript in my lap. After years in publishing, I've come to prefer manuscripts to bound books. There's a greater sense of mystery—the same white pages, the same typeface, nothing to indicate what makes the story unique. You just have to plunge in.

It doesn't take long to see that this one isn't going anywhere. The author seems to think that the futuristic setting gives him license to play any tricks he wants. At the first sign of danger, the hero can flick a switch on his wristwatch and end up on a beach in Tahiti. After a few hours of this, I'm grateful to hear the doorbell.

"Surprise!" a woman's voice squeaks through the intercom. She's certainly correct on that score.

"Who is it?"

"Christina. I've come to pick up Sarah."

"She's not—" But it isn't worth explaining through the box. I press the buzzer and wait for her to climb the stairs. It's Victor's job to pick Sarah up on Saturday and return her Sunday night. I'm sure that's today's arrangement, but Christina must have had a change of heart.

Christina's only previous appearance at the apartment, since I moved in, had more the air of an inspection than a friendly visit. Victor had invited her to dinner, to introduce me—to assure her of my qualifications as a guardian for her daughter. After all, she was entrusting Sarah to my care every other weekend; she had a right to know what she was getting herself into. Throughout dinner, though, I'd had the feeling it was less my parenting abilities that interested her than my wifely duties. I'd seen women use that look on each other—the head-to-toe analysis, the determined search for cellulite or dark roots. She wanted to know what Victor saw in me, what I had that she didn't—as if a penis weren't enough.

Even now, bursting through the half-open door in a white flash—long ivory wool coat, cascading blonde hair, shopping bags dangling from each hand—she can't resist the once-over. Her technique isn't much different from my own now-rusty cruising strategy, albeit a bit more transparent.

The *Globe* is still spread out on the sofa, Sarah's coloring book open-faced on the carpet, crayons lying haphazardly around it. Christina catches me crouching down to clean up the mess, and smiles. Tapping the sections of the paper into a single pile, I rise to meet her. She's looking expectantly around the room, the paper handles of the shopping bags pressing heavily into her palms. Finally, she sets the bags against the wall, Lord & Taylor roses sharply contrasting the white background, and shuts the door.

"Hello, Greg." She wraps the long strap of her purse around the bag and drops it onto the sofa. Her coat follows, and in a moment she's planted herself in my armchair. "How's everything?"

"Quiet," I say, replacing Sarah's crayons in their box. They leave a waxy film on my fingers, a thick odor; I'll have to wash my hands.

"I can see that. Where is everyone?"

"They went to the museum. But I had work to do." I gesture toward the manuscript on the floor beside her.

She reaches down and picks up a page. "What is it?" she asks, reading a few lines.

"Firewood."

"That bad, eh?"

I shrug. "Trees have died for worse, I suppose. There are always bodice-rippers."

She lets the page flutter back to the stack. "I used to love those old romance novels. The men were always so dashing, so sure of themselves."

"The women so weak and powerless." We sound like jacket copy. I'm still standing in the middle of the room, waiting for an explanation. She sits so placidly, one might think she'd been invited. "What are you doing in town?" I ask finally. "I thought Victor was going to drive Sarah back to Wellesley tonight."

"He was. But I had all this Christmas shopping to do, so I figured I'd save him the trouble."

"Well, I don't know when they'll be back."

"That's okay; I'll wait." She glances down at the manuscript again. "Unless you'd rather—"

"No." I pick up the entire manuscript and rewrap it in its rubber band. I'll have to lug the thing back to the office tomorrow so my assistant can return it to the author. The incinerator would be much more efficient.

"Good," she says, "then we can talk."

I can't imagine what we have to talk about. Since that dinner six months ago, our interaction has been limited to brief telephone conversations, my end consisting of, "Hi, let me get Victor for you." I prefer it that way, and I've always assumed she did, too.

"Can I get you anything?" I ask.

"You read my mind," she says. "Just a glass of wine, if you have it. I do have to drive later. Or don't you keep anything here?"

So Victor's told her that, too. Are there any secrets left? "No problem," I say, forcing a smile. "I think I can scrounge up some wine." I head into the kitchen. There's an open bottle in the fridge; Victor likes to unwind with a drink after work. Pulling out the cork, I catch a sharp whiff of the bouquet and have to stifle an urge to pour some for myself. I make Victor brush his teeth before kissing me, to lessen the temptation.

When I return, Christina has gravitated toward a corner by the window. She takes the glass, her faintly pink fingernails complementing the golden wine. "Aren't you having anything?" she asks. "I hate to drink alone."

"Maybe I'll have a Coke later."

She nods and takes a sip. Her lipstick, a perfect match for the nail polish, leaves a half-moon on the glass. "Victor always was good at picking out wine," she says.

I'm having trouble reading her expression. I'm not prepared to be sympathetic toward my lover's ex-wife, but there's something vulnerable about the turn of her lip, the way one lock of otherwise perfect hair scoops out of place by her ear. I don't know Christina; I have very little sense of her life outside those phone calls, outside Victor's biweekly visits to her house to retrieve his daughter. I never go with him on those Saturday mornings, never return with him on Sunday nights. I would be out of place somehow; he needs that time, driving back alone, to get used to the transition from having a daughter to having a lover.

Christina drinks the wine quickly, half the glass gone before she speaks again. "How's Sarah?"

"Fine. We took her to *The Nutcracker* last night."

"Yes, Victor told me you would. Did she enjoy it?"

"She loved it."

"Good. It was like pulling teeth at first to get her to take lessons, but now that's all she wants to do." Christina walks away, around the perimeter of the room, and I find myself trailing behind, as if she's leading a tour. Her eyes linger on certain objects—a brass clock on the mantel, a crystal vase Victor inherited from his grandmother. Things he's had for years, things that used to be in her house.

"Victor's wonderful with Sarah," she says. "Very attentive. Very protective."

I see Victor's hands clutching Sarah's belly, pulling her away from disease. "Yes," I whisper, "he is."

"Some men are born to be fathers. It's like he knows everything she thinks before she says it. No wonder Sarah adores him." She blinks slowly, mascara locking her lashes together for a split second.

"What are you doing for Christmas?" she asks, completing

her circuit of the room and settling back into the chair. The *you* comes out sharper, more pointed than the rest of the sentence; it's assumed that I already know *her* plans.

"Nothing," I tell her, squatting on an arm of the sofa. "I'm Jewish, remember?"

She laughs nervously. "Sorry, I forgot. Then you don't mind Sarah and me stealing Victor for the day."

Actually, I do, but Victor and I settled that argument weeks ago—or he did. "Not at all. I've never really understood the ritual anyway."

"I thought you exchanged gifts at Hanukkah." Her glass dangles from her hand, a single golden drop of wine sliding slowly toward the stem.

"It's not really the same." In grade school, the Gentile kids were always envious, assuming I got eight times the presents they did; I never bothered to disillusion them.

"Oh!" Christina blurts. "That reminds me!" Clattering her glass onto the coffee table, she scurries toward the shopping bags and begins digging through one. Paper rustles as she lifts one package after another—presents, I assume, but I wonder for whom. Does she still buy something for Victor, just so he has something to open in front of Sarah? A wallet, a wide and garish necktie—the sort of thing suburban fathers get every year. I wonder if I'll smell Brut or Old Spice on Victor's neck when he gets home Christmas night.

"Isn't this darling?" Christina cries, delicately unfolding a handful of tissue paper. She holds the tiny dress by the shoulders—blindingly white, with a lace collar and cuffs on its short sleeves. I can't imagine Sarah standing still long enough to keep it clean.

Christina turns the dress around, gazes at the collar as though picturing Sarah's head set above it. "Oh, what the hell," she says, "it's too good to hold on to. Besides, she'll have a ton of gifts to open at Christmas." Still pinching the dress at the shoulders, her other fingers extended into the air, she marches into the hall.

An unexpected territorial instinct pulls me along. I'm right behind her when she opens the door to Sarah's room. She lays the dress atop the pink and white bedspread and steps back to admire it. "I can hardly wait to see the look on her face," she says.

Christina strolls slowly to the far side of the room, studying her daughter's home away from home. She picks up Sarah's latest toy, a spongy, flexible doll that folds up into a cupcake. Christina squishes the head down, the pleated blue dress miraculously transforming into a frilly cup holder, and lays it gently on the shelf. Each time Sarah visits, there's something new—a toy, a dress, a stuffed animal. The room is already crammed with such presents, to make her feel at home, to give the apartment history for her. Victor wants to make every moment count; he may see Sarah only a few days a month, but those days must be packed with quality time, not a second wasted.

"What's this?" Christina flips through a sketch pad on the desk. The afternoon sunlight glows on the blond oak, and Christina's bracelet sparkles as she turns the pages. I draw up beside her and she shifts the book to share the pictures. They're squiggles mostly—meaningless shapes with an occasional face peering in from a corner.

"Look," Christina says, "I think that's our house." It's the typical child's A-frame, four-paned windows on each side of the door. I realize suddenly that this is as close as I'll come to seeing the real thing, the house where Victor spent five years of his life.

"I feel like a spy," Christina says. "Sarah never lets me see her drawings."

The next page at first seems just as conventional—stick

figures holding hands, a family. A child is in the center, denoted female by virtue of curly hair and a triangular purple skirt. On her right, the mother, with the same features but much larger. The father's on the other side, no curls, no triangles, the round chin garlanded by a full beard. And beside him—Christina and I both notice it at the same moment, I can feel our eyes turning together to stare—another figure, identical except for the beard. There's no caption, no names to describe the characters. She doesn't need names to identify her family.

The front door suddenly creaks open, Sarah's voice arching into the air. She's singing again—a new song, something upbeat and charmingly unrecognizable. Christina quickly closes the sketch pad, as if afraid of being caught spying, and we walk out of the room together.

We're standing side by side in the hall when Sarah notices us. Victor, kneeling down, is helping her out of her coat, pulling her arms free of the sleeves. "Mommy!" she cries. "Guess what we did today!" She runs across the room, her tiny boots carving *U*-shaped indentations in the carpet, and stops, breathless, between Christina and me. With one arm around Christina's left leg and the other around my right, she leans back to look up at us, turning her head from one to the other, as though she can't make up her mind, as though she wants equal and complete attention from us both.

Her grip is firm, fingers pressing sharply into my denimed thigh. There's a delicate passion in her touch. If she lets go, if either of us pulls away, she'll fall back onto the carpet, like crayons spilled from a box. Already, Sarah knows about the fragility of family, the bonds that can so easily, so unexpectedly, break.

I look up at her father by the door, Sarah's empty coat limp in his hands. He seems as shocked as I am by her sudden show of indiscriminate love. Sarah trembles excitedly beneath me, her energy pulsing out as if to take us all in, to draw the three of us together around her. Victor stares, and suddenly his features soften again. I know that look, like ice melting, like hearts opening. I know.

BROODING INTERVALS

Kevin Langson

I could discern Mohsen's recent mood by the size of his orgasm. We'd been meeting for sex, and increasingly, a bit of conversation and commiseration, for roughly six months, and I knew there to be a correlation between his level of joy and the frequency with which he got off. When his sensitive mind was too addled with the afflictions he only alluded to, his neglected sperm congregated and formed a restive mass ready to be unleashed at my hands.

Mohsen had appeared shivering at the entrance to my decrepit apartment building, his tender and tentative grin obscured by a faux-fur-trimmed hood pulled tight. San Francisco's weather is as defiant of expectations as a transient offspring in a bourgeois family (which both of us were), but that February afternoon was true winter. I imagined I was offering him refuge from a journey through a Siberian-scale tundra of gay indifference. I was compelled to lean down and find his thin lips within the hood, but I resisted.

It was fleetingly pleasing when his nearly ethereal groan gave way to an effusive spewing, yet I was aware of the implications as his semen fell on my chin, collarbone and chest. I was no stranger to postcoital melancholia myself, but his shift was alarming. Shivers quelled, moans silenced, face fallen; his delight gave way to what could only be deemed abjection, as if his erection was all that could keep it at bay. I knew it was time to rise from my knees to get a towel or rag; that was the protocol. But I was inert with the acknowledgment that the pleasure we arrived at together could so soon be whisked away.

He insisted on seeing me through to orgasm, like a soldier propelled by a vague conviction in his war, despite a despairing heart. From the very edge of my ragged mattress on the floor I reached to grasp his buttocks as he used his spit-glistening hand to stroke me. I focused on the white of his lips where his bite chased the blood away, then the dark stubble that toughened his visage. His gaze drifted between my eyes and my groin but never lost concentration.

Afterward, he stood nude by the window of my small studio apartment, his receding dick pointing downward toward jostling dealers and junkies, as well as wary civilians swerving to avoid proximity or stepping on waste. At all hours, Turk Street teemed with the unsavory interactions the Tenderloin was infamous for—drugs sold, inner demons unleashed, racial resentment rabidly articulated, hipsters spat on, sidewalks shat on. I sometimes recoiled, but I adored it. It disheartened me less than the glittering windows of trendy boutiques born out of late-stage gentrification.

"*Mamnoon,*" he muttered, turning away from the window. He always thanked me in Farsi, a small concession to my likely annoying request that he speak his native language to me during intimacy. It wasn't a lascivious desire, like getting off on a muscled German guy gruffly declaring, "*Ich werde dich hart ficken,*" as he pounds away at his blissful American booty.

Farsi lulled me into a poetic mind, a sense of artful languor.

"How can you live here?" he asked. I had joined him at the window, and from the fifth floor we watched a banal scuffle of Tenderloin hooligans. A spasmodic woman spread her puffy red coat to ensconce a wiry man as he moved to and fro like a withering menace.

"Does she wish to smother that guy with her vile coat?" Mohsen wondered aloud.

"How can you live in Oakland?" I replied to his initial question. "I still contend it's better to live at the hard knock center of SF—street feces and used syringes and all—than to commute from Oaktown any time something worthwhile is happening in the city. You might as well be in suburbia, for all the spontaneity and splendor that the Oak allows."

Once, in the abbreviated chats that followed sex, we'd lamented being downwardly mobile. We were poverty poseurs of sorts during university; then we were sincerely impoverished in the art school and liberal arts aftermath, which was far too common an affliction in a city designed for moneyed progressives. I'd lived in the Mission, the epicenter of bohemia, while on my parents' bill and had hastily vacated after graduating. All of this was dull, I felt, next to Mohsen's trajectory. As I admired him in repose, it required a student's discipline not to assault him with a deluge of questions. He'd once referred to the Curious Caucasian Syndrome, scoffing at the questions posed by his lovers at the revelation of his Persian ethnicity. Listening, I felt like a foolish old john who convinces himself he's an exception in claiming the affections of his favorite whore.

Mohsen stared down at the street as if all the world was inscrutable and he could only venture to be amused from afar. Small patches of soft black hair accentuated his pecs, and coarser hair led up his soccer-player legs to an ass that was surprisingly hairless until you got to the edge of the crack, where hair dense and dark like the depths of a northern forest drew one's eyes to that crevice. I was smitten.

Ordinarily, my stares were cautious, as I'd numerous times been embarrassed when caught, but with Mohsen I relaxed. He stared unabashedly—sometimes at me, causing me to squirm, sometimes at the objects and spaces that made up my home. He turned slowly toward me, as if trying to draw a connection between what was happening on the street and me, and I again caught a glimpse of the unfathomable in his eyes. Sometimes they shimmered with intimate promise; other times they seemed to feign vacancy so that I wouldn't bother trying to penetrate his thoughts. I hadn't truly tried. I no longer trusted my perception of profundity. I'd so many times swooned for some force or curled up beside some warmth that soon revealed itself to be illusory. San Francisco was a city of transient affections.

Mohsen listlessly ran a finger over the window ledge, and then seemed to scrutinize the sizable ball of dust that had collected at its tip. "Suicide doesn't suit me," he said simply, as if it were a logical continuation of a conversation we'd been having.

"Well, um, I'm glad for that."

He looked down at the dirty windowsill. I thought, *Why don't I ever clean anything?*

"I mean, it seems like a perfectly legitimate response in the absolute absence of hope, but it's just too dramatic, desperate—like a play for a headline or for pity and regret from people who haven't considered me in ages."

His curt laugh emanated from the outskirts of lunacy. "Suicide. My strongest association with it is a bit absurd. The first lover I took when I moved to the Bay Area was an underhanded motherfucker—Michael. One afternoon, after a romp of foreplay, he pulled a sad face and said he had something horrible to tell me. He said he dreaded it like his father's cooking, but he just had to be honest with me. Then he told me that he was HIV positive. In the ten or twelve minutes before he conceded it was just a fabrication to test my empathy, my mind raced through a million morbid thoughts, the final one being that the poor lad would commit suicide. He was already self-loathing; he wouldn't be able to cope." He laughed again and looked over at me. "I actually felt homicidal toward him. I left his apartment and never contacted him again."

I thought of the Craigslist ad I'd stumbled across a few months ago in which a young guy had threatened to off himself if he didn't get "blasted with at least ten loads" up his "slut ass" by the end of that night. I'd wondered if I should notify the police. It seemed callous to ignore that but also lame and intrusive to call the authorities. Now I wondered if anyone else intervened, or if he got his coveted loads.

Suddenly my thoughts shifted to what Mohsen was like with his other lovers. Was he safe? Was he rough? Did he tend toward domination, as he did with me? Was there the same complicated interplay of tenderness and sullenness?

He rose and walked over to the tiny kitchen in the right corner of my open square of a home. He opened a cupboard and sifted through my boxes of herbal tea, not seeming to find anything to his liking. Though it was the first time that he'd made himself at home in any part of my apartment other than my mattress, it seemed natural somehow.

I said, "When I was about eight and my sister announced that she was going to vet school, I was horrified, and I pleaded with her to choose another path and with my mother not to let her, much to the dismay of both of them. I had seen enough ratty guys by the highway holding cardboard signs that said HOMELESS VET that I figured she was fated to become a mistress of the streets."

He turned the knob to ignite the flame of the back burner, occupied by my black kettle, and then turned toward me without looking directly at me. "I'm sure there's a reason you are telling me this, but it eludes me," he said without unkindness. He turned back to the counter to prepare his pomegranate tea.

"I'm prone to being concerned for people I care for, though it's sometimes misguided or awkwardly expressed."

I watched minute shudders ripple across his backside. I pulled down the burgundy afghan from the top shelf of my closet and draped it over his shoulders as he poured honey. Timorously, I kissed the spot above his collarbone where a few stray hairs sprouted. I found it strange. Moments earlier we'd been swept up in a brazen, wet sex embrace that was beastly and gentle, in turns. But now this gesture brought a tremble to me. I half-expected him to pull away.

He stood still and the plastic honey bear tipped, leaking a fine drizzle, not unlike his relaxing cock after ejaculation or at the onset of arousal.

"It's going to be too sweet," I warned in a whisper, nodding toward the honey.

He laughed lightly. "It's too bad this isn't a cheesy movie because then I could say something like, '*You're* too sweet, my dear,' and I'd let the honey continue to pour." He placed the honey bear back on the counter.

"You can say whatever you like with me," I said simply.

"Okay. That is borderline. Well, I'll take it because I think I believe in its sincerity." He blew on his tea, and then looked into the pot that occupied the front burner. With an exaggerated expression of disgust he pulled out a soggy mess of ramen noodles that I had forgotten and left to turn to mush. He clicked in disapproval as he lifted them out and threatened, with a gesture, to throw them on my head, but instead carried them to the window, opened it, and tossed the soppy mass down onto the sidewalk—or perhaps on the head of a hapless passerby. "Ruffians like ramen," he announced, turning back to me.

"Maybe, but no one likes someone else's mush."

"Absolutely true. It was a painful lesson for me to learn, that keeping my mush to myself is less agonizing than the indignity of sharing with someone who is banefully indifferent."

He sat on the dog-shredded brown-and-burgundy rug by my mattress, touching in turn a cluster of objects as if he were an infant learning textures—a small pile of half-written postcards to friends back East and overseas, Band-Aids, and an Aleksandar Hemon novel I sometimes quoted to him because I thought he, as an immigrant, could appreciate the wit of the Bosnian cum Chicagoan author.

He picked up a postcard addressed to Tayfun and read in a low voice, squinting to decipher my tiny print, "This city is too sexual; I can't tune it out. I miss the arduous pursuits of Istanbul. Sex shouldn't be too easy, too readily available. Don't you agree? Still, I hope you have found a lover, someone worthy of your singular spirit." Placing the postcard back on the floor, he looked at me. "Do you think he will understand that? The vocabulary, I mean?"

"Tayfun revels in having reason to pull out the petite yellow dictionary he carries around."

"I wore out numerous petite dicts when I was in grad school. Now I can knock almost any American guy down in a vocab fight." He made a boxing gesture, punching my shoulder and pushing me back on the mattress. "Even you, I bet, word-nerd white boy," he whispered, hovering above my face.

I reached my hand around the back of his neck and pulled him down on top of me, with a wide goofy smile like the kind I stifled when being photographed. "My sexy word fighter." My words came out with a subtle romantic flourish that frightened me upon hearing it. I grabbed his groin. "Your big vocabulary more than compensates for—" He let loose a long string of drool and clenched my jaw still so that I couldn't squirm to avoid it. I didn't really want to anyhow. As his spit snaked its way down from my lower lip to my chin, then my Adam's apple, he rose off of me, and when he brought his gaze back to my lustful one, his eyes glinted with rage.

"Yours?" he asked forcefully, observing my befuddlement. "*Your* fighter?"

My confusion gave way to embarrassment. In my playful spirit, I'd spoken as if the world was of my design. It was an embellishment of our connection. Unconsciously, I'd laid some tentative claim on him, not a possessing but an acknowledgment that we offered to each other some experience that circumvented the trappings of other lovers; at least those were my unexamined sentiments.

Ordinarily I withdrew from any hostility or threat of confrontation. But his anger, even more than it confused me, captivated me. His unflinching gaze was a warped sort of gift whose unwrapping required cunning.

Finally I looked over at the tiny clock beside my mattress and thought out loud, "This is the longest you have stayed," then watched the subtle storm of his countenance like a neophyte scientist.

"Do you want me to leave?"

I turned to the window, as if the answer were in the balmy evening light, sunlight draining in concordance with the simplicity of our relations. There was so much about him to untangle: his animosity toward his parents, his homeland and America—all only mentions between critical sighs. I was somehow certain that his ambivalence toward San Francisco was akin to my own and that there was something beneath his brooding that justified it.

But my experience in romance was like his in his nations of residence; I knew the pitfalls, the statistical likelihood of disappointment and even the possibility of despair if too much was ventured. It was like interrogating a suspected terrorist who could either blow you up or be the inspiration for your memoir.

As I turned back to the room, my eyes passed over my laptop on the desk in the corner. "I have an article to revise," I said.

When he rose, standing atop my mattress like the somber prince of a precarious pile of rubble, I thought he was preparing to get dressed and leave, but he let the afghan fall from his body and stood motionless for a moment. "Do you know why I hate this color?" he asked, indicating the afghan. I shook my head. "It's like the crimson of Harvard."

"Do you have a personal vendetta against Harvard?"

"When I was a junior in high school, my parents insisted I apply to Harvard and other such bullshit institutions, completely ignoring my explanations that they weren't even renowned for illustration, what I wanted to study. It didn't matter what I wanted. They only wanted some easy-to-articulate prestige for their son. All I wanted was California and art that gives a potent fuck-you to propriety, which to them meant I could go to Stanford and take a literature elective. I even considered flying back to Iran just to undo everything they did for me. That was going to be my contemptuous living suicide, my Persian version of the American bottom slut who opens up his ass to HIV."

I imagined my hastened heartbeat was percussion for his monologue. Despite the fact that he appeared to be onstage with me his audience of one, there was no aura of performance in his delivery. He was watching for my response. I was still terrified and rapt when he continued.

"I've only taken raw cock once outside of dating, and it was exhilarating and frightening. Three buddies took turns with me in Buena Vista Park, and even as it was happening I was sickened by my delight. Kind of like my feelings for this city—a wild rush of visceral elation, interrupted in intervals by revulsion. As the last guy was finishing with me, I checked my watch and realized I would miss the last train. I just rolled over and cried myself to sleep in the park. I woke at dawn to a homeless man grumbling, 'Hey kid, someone stole your shoes.' I hadn't worn socks, and I recall stepping on slimy fried-chicken bones seemingly all the way from Haight down to Sixteenth. I started laughing like a fucking loony, embracing the disgusting cold feeling between my toes, and fantasizing that there was a form of lobotomy that could eviscerate libido. I wanted it gone. I felt like I could deal with my penchant for destructive behavior without lust. Lust is what really fucks things up."

I stared into the dark hair of his chest, wanting to capture and keep his confession in some solid form, wanting to tell him I had had the same sentiments about lust, wanting most of all to respond. But the moment could only be degraded by anything I said.

He relaxed his stance and watched me. He was entering one of the brooding intervals I had come to take as his trademark, a louder version of what invariably overtook him after we got off. I thought, *How does such a sullen boy make any tips as a waiter?*

He squatted in front of me, the lowering sun caressing the crown of his head. It occurred to me it was peculiar that we were still nude despite the chill. "Did you mean what you said before?" he asked.

"What?"

"That I could say whatever to you."

"Of course." I bit my lip, brushed a crumb of something from my toe. "I've grown awkwardly fond of you, Mohsen."

His smile dissipated as abruptly as it had appeared. "Why is it awkward?"

"Well, it's not necessary for what we have. I mean, we respect each other and find each other hot. It seems there's no room for anything else in the equation."

He rose to his feet and stepped down off the mattress with a thud. Then he was carving a jagged path around my studio, as if clumsily encircling prey. Was this his way of controlling rage? Some obscure part of me rebelled against my own passivity. I was inept at getting at what I really wanted from someone like Mohsen—the difficult narrative, the tenebrous bits he wouldn't utter to other lovers and the chance to be a counterforce. Fucking wasn't enough, even with tinges of tenderness.

I heard his foot colliding with my closet door.

"It's always the same in this fucking country. I can't explain this feeling to you. It's that every consolation that has gotten me through is empty. The goddamn people here—there is the guy I go to Occupy protests with, the punk I get drunk with, the Daddy I let fuck me like an animal and treat me to overpriced dinners, the workmate I bitch and moan about obnoxious customers with, then there's you."

I backed up against the wall, beneath the window. He seemed to be gauging how hurtful he wanted to be.

"You are the gentle fuckbuddy. A little conversation thrown in to make it more reasonable, less animalistic, sex that isn't just fucking but isn't quite lovemaking. Dead-end caresses, but fabulous orgasms." He said fabulous as if mocking all of gay identity.

He moved toward me but ended up in the corner by my desk. He glanced at my laptop as if he wanted to thrash it against the wall; instead, he turned toward the wall and thrust his fist into it as if exorcising a murderous will.

He turned as he spoke. "I can't do it anymore. I just need one whole person. Not a fucking husband but one whole person I can spend a day with—eat, shit, wake up, fight the world, get wasted, get sober, sleep beside. One person who can stick around long enough to get a different fucking view."

His eyes, spilling rage, were like black funnels grasping for my response. In the same way one laughs at a funeral, I found myself fixating on an image of us shitting in unison, then climbing down the fire escape, our britches still down, and waddling to the Civic Center for a protest. I still felt impotent and absurd, but through it all I knew there was something strong rising to my surface. Mohsen's rage was a challenge.

He approached, bent down and gingerly took my left nipple between his fingers as if preparing to twist hard. I shut my eyes, recalling having told him about my profound dread of nipple pain. His stillness allowed my fear, lust and affection to comingle in an odd moment before he continued. "I don't want you if you're like the others. What is the use in being outwardly strange if you're really just the same?" I cut my eyes toward the window when I heard a siren on Turk Street. "Silence is not an option this time, fuckhead," he declared as he intensified his hold on my nipple.

I relaxed the squinting muscles of my eyes. The sensation of his fingers softly grasping my nipple, not pinching but not releasing, felt like a tender subversion. He was waiting. I leaned my head into his chest, blowing my hot breath on his chest hair, like a taut summer breeze ruffling reed grass. "Spend the night and tomorrow with me. I'm going to a demonstration downtown. We can eat a nice meal on the way, moan about puerile people, fuck like animals and finish with the whiskey in my cupboard."

DANDELIONS

Tony Calvert

My nightmares are wallpapered in pale blue with little pink roses.

Wait; it wasn't a nightmare. I was at my mother's house. It was eight A.M. She was right outside the door vacuuming. This was real. All too real.

What right-thinking woman would be vacuuming at eight A.M.? I stumbled out of bed and threw open the door to confront Lilah Lynn Hutton with her villainy.

She didn't miss a beat. "Morning Jimmy. We have guests coming this afternoon, so we have to get the place ready."

"Morning, Mom."

She grimaced. "Honestly, you look like you've been on a three-day bender. Take a shower. Breakfast in twenty minutes."

I nodded and closed the door. That hadn't gone as I'd planned.

"Don't forget to brush your teeth!"

It wasn't her reminding me to brush my teeth that annoyed

me so much; it was the singsong way she said it that got me.

My move back to Mississippi to live with my mother hadn't been high on my "to do" list. I had two brothers and a sister, all living the American Dream, all married, all with children, all living their lives elsewhere. I was single. I was a writer. I was gay. When it came to taking care of Mom and Dad in their golden years, I was everyone's obvious choice; nothing held me to one place.

But I hadn't expected it to happen so soon.

My father had died three months before. He and Mom had gone to dinner with Max and Ellen Avery. When he started complaining about chest pains, my mother thought he was faking it. I got that; the Averys were pretty gruesome in a smug, country-club way. Everything happened fast. Dad passed away before Mom was even able to call to let any of us know he was in the hospital.

As soon as I heard, I knew I was leaving Atlanta. I was going back to my old home, back to my old room and back to a life I didn't want. I was trying to make the best of it, and I wasn't sure that was working.

"You can write anywhere. Mom needs the help. It's not like you have anything else going on," Tom, my oldest brother, had said at the funeral. His words made me angry, mainly because they were true. In a few years I'd be forty; I wrote historical romances under an assumed name and I'd never been in love. I didn't have anything going on.

Standing in the shower for an extra ten minutes wasn't going to wash that feeling off.

Mom believed in a big breakfast, at least for other people. She'd made me a mess of SOS, and no one appreciated chipped beef and gravy over toast like me. Mom picked at her muffin while I ate.

"We have a lot to do today. It's the first time we'll have guests since your father passed."

When I'd first left home, my brothers and sister had been concerned that Lilah Lynn and good old Frank were going to have problems with the empty nest thing. That hadn't been the case. As soon as I was in the car, Frank and Lilah Lynn were traveling. They hit every bed-and-breakfast in the South. When they returned home, they began remodeling the house, and two years later they were the proud proprietors of The Dandy Lyons Inn.

Tourism had boomed in my little hometown. The secondhand stores and junk shops from my childhood were now antique boutiques. Small galleries filled with the work of local painters. Folk art ruled, with new festivals and craft fairs that hadn't been around when I'd left. It was impossible to walk downtown without seeing a painted gourd in a store window. The Dandy Lyons Inn was cashing in.

Three couples were arriving that weekend. Mom scribbled on her notepad and said, "We'll have pecan pie and cornbread for dinner, of course." She dropped her voice to a whisper even though we were the only two in the house. "They're all from up North; they'll expect that."

Apparently having Yankees in the house was something we still had to keep from the neighbors.

"What says welcome more, chicken and dumplings or fried chicken and okra?"

I thought for a moment. "Fried chicken and okra: isn't that too much fried?"

"Good point. Chicken and dumplings it is. You're like your father; he always knew what we should serve."

She'd finished her muffin and gone into the kitchen.

"Not really. I just love chicken and dumplings."

"Just like your father," she called back as I shoved in another mouthful.

I considered that. SOS. Chicken and dumplings. I needed to start working out.

Lilah sat back down, fresh cup of coffee in her hand. "All three couples are newlyweds. That's so exciting!"

I kept eating.

"Jimmy, don't roll your eyes at me."

I wasn't aware that I had.

"Mom, most people call me Jim now, because you know, I'm a man, not a twelve-year-old."

"If there's one thing I never understood, it's why you have such a disdain for love."

"What? I don't have a disdain for love. I write about love. I'm all about love! I *am* love!"

She put her cup down. "No, *Avalon Dupre* is all about love. Jimmy Hutton is scared of it. I have to tell you: Avalon Dupre is the most ridiculous name. Where did you get that?"

"Lots of people like Avalon Dupre." It was true. I wasn't a best seller, but I made a pretty decent living from writing historicals, or *hystericals* as Tom called them.

"And why do you refer to her like she's real?" She pursed her lips the way she always did when she thought she was making a good point. "*You're* Avalon Dupre. Have you ever wondered why you write all those dramatic love stories?"

"I wouldn't call them dramatic."

"Anything that features pirates is dramatic."

"One pirate. I've only done the pirate thing *once*."

"What's the one you're writing now?"

"It's titled *Under the Gypsy Moon.*"

"You don't think pirates and gypsies are just a tinge dramatic?"

"Mom..." I really didn't want to explain my writing to her, especially at breakfast after I'd been awakened by a vacuum cleaner.

"I'm just saying. I think you write these *sweeping* love stories because that's what you're looking for. You and your sister Valerie have always had these grand expectations. That's why she's been married three times and you've never made it down the aisle once."

"Or maybe because it isn't legal."

"Love can be a very quiet thing."

I knew she was thinking of Dad. I considered her judgment of my sister and me. It might be true that Valerie was looking for the dramatic; certainly she'd married some swindling jackasses who were missing a few teeth. But I wrote about a betrayed, justice-seeking pirate with a heart of gold in *The Scoundrel Takes a Mistress,* and all I'd ever wanted was a love story like my parents'.

Frank and Lilah were introduced on a blind date arranged by friends who thought they'd complement each other. Frank Hutton was reserved and quiet, and Lilah Lynn Lyons was a force of nature, free spirited and wild. The night ended when my mother danced in the fountain in the center of town during a rainstorm. Frank fell in love. They were married for almost fifty years, and they never stopped dating. When a kid grew up bearing witness to the world's greatest romance, it was hard not to want the same thing.

Lilah swooped in and took my plate. "Let's go. How many times do I need to tell you we have lots to do?"

Our first errand was at a craft store, where we picked up items for our guests' gift baskets. At the liquor store, she bought a few bottles of champagne and her box of sangria. Then we went to the bakery and the grocery store, where I had my revenge. There was someone on every aisle eager to strike up a conversation, and I kept the cart moving and reminded her, "Lots to do!"

The nursery was the last place on her list.

"What's the name of this place?"

"You remember Daisy Ludo, right? She owned the flower shop on Market Street, Daisy Mayhems; they were a little too high priced for my liking." Mom always took the long way around a question. "When Marv retired—Marv is her husband—they asked their nephew to take over—he's some kind of plant genius—while they traveled for a year in their RV. When they got back, he started this nursery. They have the best plants here. Affordable, too." She lowered her voice. "I know that has to drive Daisy crazier than ever. You know how everyone in town calls her Crazy Daisy. She has a little shop in the back."

"So what's the name?" I asked again.

"Soil and Green."

"Oh, that's good." I laughed. She stared at me, and I knew she didn't get the homage to the sci-fi classic starring Charlton Heston. The Ludo nephew had a sense of humor.

I followed Mom into the greenhouse and then to the garden, where she called, "Eric?"

A man with shaggy blond hair and blue eyes came out of the greenery. He was wearing khaki cargo pants, an olive-green T-shirt and a shark-tooth necklace. He looked more like a surfer than a—I stumbled over the term. What exactly did you call a guy who owned a nursery? Avalon Dupre had never written a novel about horticulture.

He smiled immediately when he saw my mom. "Mrs. Hutton, I was going to call to see if I could come to the inn with the azaleas."

It was weird to hear my childhood home referred to as "the inn."

"I just came by to pick up a few things. Oh—and I wanted to introduce you to my son." She looked back at me, her eyes sparkling with mischief. "This is Jimmy." She sighed dramatically. "Or am I supposed to call you James now? I never know."

"Jimmy is fine, Mom."

"Are you sure?" I knew the question was rhetorical and didn't answer. "He's my youngest; I think you two are close to the same age. He grew up here, but things have changed so much since then. Maybe you could get together and go out, Eric, and you could show him all your hangouts."

It was the enthusiasm in her voice that clued me in. Eric was gay. This was a setup.

"Mom..."

Eric smiled. "Anything I can do to help, Mrs. Hutton."

"I'm going to talk to your aunt about flowers, and you"—she poked me in the stomach—"talk with Eric about delivering my azaleas. And whatever else you want to talk about."

We both watched as she sashayed toward the back of the greenhouse.

"Your mom's a pistol." Eric smiled, shaking his head.

"Yeah, she's something," I mumbled.

His face was serious. "I'm sorry about your father; he was a really nice man. They came in here a lot. He always was holding your mom's hand, not just here, but any time I saw them in town."

I nodded. "Yeah, they were pretty incredible together." No one missed how in love my parents were. I cleared my throat. "So you like science fiction?"

Eric laughed. "I love that movie! I'm glad you caught that. Your mom talks about you all the time. She was excited about you staying on. Are you liking it?"

Dalton Springs was no Atlanta, but it wasn't like I'd done a lot of "big city" things when I lived there. "I'm still getting used to things. It's changed a lot, gotten a little busier, but it's still quiet. That works for a writer. Although I'm not sure about living in a bed-and-breakfast. There's always something that needs doing."

"Your mom wanted some dwarf azaleas and a mimosa tree for that bare spot in the front yard. I tried to talk her out of it; I worry about the webworms."

"My dad loved mimosa trees."

He groaned. "Well now I feel assy."

"Don't; I'm sure she appreciated that you were looking out for her." I changed the subject to something more comfortable. "When I lived in Atlanta, I had a ponytail palm. I left it with my neighbor. I'd love to have another one."

"I'm sure I have one here. It'll take me a second to find it."

Mom crept up on us like a spider. "What are we finding?"

"Jimmy wants a ponytail palm."

"I need something to make my room seem like mine again."

"You have a gorgeous room." She sniffed.

"It's been shabby chic-ed to death."

"I couldn't leave all your stuff up. No one would want to stay in the 'Woe is me, I like everything dark and spooky, Edgar Allan Poe room.'" She looked at Eric and whispered, "He went through a goth phase. His father and I were so concerned."

"It wasn't a goth thing. I—" I caught Eric chuckling. "Never mind."

My mother handed me a bouquet of sunflowers, daisies, lilies and pink roses. "These are for the living room, under the painting. Did you give Eric your phone number?" She smiled her *I'm just a sweet old Southern lady* smile at Eric. "Maybe *you* can get him to go somewhere other than the library."

"I'll come by this afternoon with your azaleas. I'll work on him then."

"And you'll stay for dinner." It was done. Lilah Lynn had proclaimed it. She patted my shoulder. "Let's go. We have lots to do at home."

I sat in the dining room putting together gift baskets for the honeymooners who would be arriving in the next few hours. A bottle of champagne with two glasses, chocolates, postcards from town, stamps, a few brochures, and a jar of blackberry preserves that my mom had made herself.

"So, this Eric thing," I began.

She peeked into the dining room. "Isn't he a doll? It was either you or Valerie. Well, not really, I love your sister, but I don't know that I'd set her up with anyone. Remember that boy Robbie Miller she dated? I swear he's never been the same. He sees me coming down the street and turns the other way. She can destroy a good man. Besides, Eric's gay. He's more your type."

"Matchmaking is your thing now?"

"If someone doesn't help you, it's never going to happen. I'm taking the wheel. Eric is perfect for you."

"He's too..." I was about to say good-looking. Good-looking always made me a mass of goo. "Earthy. I don't do earthy. I like TV and couches."

"You and your daddy used to go fishing all the time. You can be earthy."

"Just because we're both gay doesn't mean—"

"No one knows you like your mother. You should learn to listen to me. Take those up to the rooms."

The fix-up was on. The conversation was over, at least for Lilah.

I put the gift baskets in place, checked back with Lilah Lynn, who was going to town on her pies, and sat down to write. Things weren't going well for my guys in *Under the Gypsy*

Moon. My heroine was in the arms of the handsome scoundrel Rodrigo.

"Jimmy! Eric's here to see you."

That woman!

I left my desk and ran down the stairs because I was frustrated with her, not because I wanted to see Eric in all his surfer-esque glory. At least that's what I told myself.

I found them in the kitchen. Eric was holding a ponytail palm. I really liked his smile.

"I told you I could find one somewhere in the back of my jungle." He handed it to me. "Consider it a welcome home gift."

"Thanks."

I was searching for something else to say when my mom snatched the palm out of my hands. "I'll take this up to your room. Why don't you help Eric take the azaleas to the back patio?"

I followed Eric to his truck, where he handed me a small azalea bush with pink flowers. "They're trying to get mimosas on the forbidden plants list, so I don't carry them. I had to special order it, but Lilah will have it soon."

I led him through the living room on the way to the back porch.

"Wow."

He'd stopped in front of the fireplace, staring at what everyone in my family called "the painting." My father was an amateur painter, and not a very good one, but on occasion he could knock one out of the park. "The painting" was officially titled *Dandelions Dance at Midnight,* and that's exactly what it was: a field of dandelions and a midnight sky filled with shooting stars. There was something about the colors, something that showed movement. If you looked long enough you'd swear that the dandelions really were dancing.

"My dad painted that. It's my mom. Well, metaphorically."

He nodded. "I got that. It's beautiful. Do you think a painting of dandelions can grant a wish?"

"I never tried it." I shrugged.

"You should."

"Maybe I will."

Ah, the awkward silence, only this one didn't seem so awkward. I had the urge to reach for his hand. I was grateful I had an arm full of azaleas.

He smiled. "I should get these out to the patio; Miss Lilah reminded me that guests will be arriving soon."

I led him out the back door. My parents had built a gorgeous stone patio, complete with a fire pit, when they remade our house into an inn.

"How can a mimosa be a forbidden plant?" No matter where I was, when I saw a mimosa I felt like I was home. I loved them just like my father had.

"They consider it a weed tree." He took the azalea from me. "*They* being the Mississippi Plant Board, not me. I like mimosas. They attract pollinating insects and add nutrients to the soil. They're like dandelions." He put the azaleas down and motioned toward the door. "I need to get more stuff out of the truck."

I nodded. "I should get back to my writing."

I watched as he left the house and then raced up the stairs. My mother was on the top landing.

"That plant looks very nice on your desk. It was sweet of Eric to give it to you rather than adding it to the bill, don't you think? I hope you thanked him."

"Yes, Mom." A week earlier, I'd discovered that my voice often regressed into sullen teen territory. This was one of those times.

“I opened the windows in your room; you have the best view of the backyard.” She was singsonging again. “Remember: listen to your mother, she knows best.”

I went back to my desk and started writing, determined not to look out the window. Naturally my eyes betrayed me. Eric looked good out there, drudging away under Lilah’s instruction. I made the occasional covert glance, well aware that Lilah would be looking up to see if I was looking down. After she left the patio, it was easier to take more leisurely glances. I might’ve even stared a few times, and of course I was caught. Eric smiled and waved at me. I had no choice but to wave back.

I’d churned out a few pages when there was a knock at the door.

“Since when do you knock?” No matter how old we were, the rule at the Hutton house was that Mom had an open-door policy; she could open any door she wanted. The rules were the same at The Dandy Lyons Inn.

“I always knock.” Eric was standing in the doorway. He looked around my room. “This is quite the rosy little paradise.”

“I think we both know the ‘Woe is me, I like everything dark and spooky, Edgar Allan Poe room’ would definitely sell out. Maybe to a different clientele than she’s used to. She sold everything in my room in a yard sale, including my Star Wars action figures and the Darth Vader carrying case that I inherited from Tom. She even sold Han Solo! Despite the fact that when I came out, one of the things that made it easier for her was our mutual love of Harrison Ford.”

“I’m an Indiana Jones man myself. I’m sure she wouldn’t mind if you got a few Poe posters and did a little redecorating.”

I groaned. “I swear it was not a goth thing. I loved his writing.”

He laughed. “She said I could use your bathroom to clean up

for dinner." He held up a gym bag. "I brought clean clothes."

"You don't have to stay. There's no reason we both have to endure dinner with a crazy woman."

"Are you kidding? I've been looking forward to it all day." He walked into the bathroom, leaving the door cracked a smidge, and turned on the shower. "I hear her dumplings are delicious."

"They are." So now a plant-loving surfer was naked and showering just feet away from me. I couldn't believe she was doing this to me. I called out, "I hear Yankees in the kitchen. I'd better get down there and see how Mom's handling the invasion."

By the time Eric joined us, crisp New England accents were indeed filling the house. As always, my mom was laying on the Southern charm and our guests were eating her up with two spoons.

When we sat down for dinner, one of the women mentioned how sweet it was that the first night at such a cute little bed-and-breakfast included dinner. My mother beamed. By my count, Dalton Springs was referred to as "cute" and "quaint" eighty-three times. Eric's knee hit mine each and every time, so it didn't bother me.

They all wanted to see the craft fair in Mount Eagle, and my mother made sure they had every flyer put out by every shop and gallery in town. After dinner, everyone went out on the patio, stopping to look at "the painting," and I could hear the love in my mother's voice when she talked about how it was my father's. She was definitely going to join the Saturday Night Widows' Club that met at the Blue Moon Bar to drink and ogle men. She was also going to love Dad forever.

"Hey, no offense to your mom, but I really hate pecan pie. How about we go out for a cup of coffee," Eric whispered as we cleared the table.

I nodded. "We have to make our escape before she notices."

We slipped out, making small talk as we walked. Downtown was still bustling. A horse and carriage stood in front of what I always considered my mother's fountain. We turned into Coop's Café.

The man behind the counter gave us a wave, and we sat at one of the corner tables, ordered our coffee—and there was that not-so-awkward silence again.

I pointed to one of the bar stools at the counter. "When I was a little boy, every Saturday morning my dad would bring me here. He'd have coffee with his friends, I would get a hamburger, and he'd always buy me two comic books."

"Archie?"

"I, Vampire. And any other scary comic available. I had to hide them at home so my mom wouldn't find them."

The waitress gave us our drinks. As soon as she left, Eric asked, "Is that what you write?"

"Horror?" I shook my head.

Eric waited a moment. "Care to share what you do write?"

I could feel my cheeks redden. I wanted to impress Eric. Writing historical romances wouldn't do the trick, but I wasn't going to lie. "Romances. Historical romances." As Lilah would, I whispered the rest. "I write under the name Avalon Dupre."

Eric's eyes widened and he grabbed my hand. "My mother loves you! You'll sign a book for me, right?"

I nodded. "Of course."

He didn't let go of my hand as he smiled at me. "Romance, huh?"

"Mom thinks it's because I'm looking for a sweeping romance, but that's not it. I just like the idea of something that lasts forever."

"Do you write from experience?"

"If you're asking if I've ever been in the embrace of the illegitimate son of a French nobleman, no. I'm better at writing about love than being in love."

"There's something good about being a late bloomer. Trust me; it's my area of expertise." He paused. "And hey, pirates are hot."

"Amen to that." I started to smile even though I was embarrassed by my confession. More than anything I wanted to take the focus off of me. "So what's with you and the plants? You look like a surfer."

"I moved here from California, and I have surfed. So I guess that works. I've always enjoyed being outside, gardening, stuff like that. It seemed like the right thing for me. You can tell a lot about people by the plants they like. For instance, ponytail palms. They're unique, quirky, fun and slow to grow. But they're sturdy. They last."

"Are you calling me slow?" He smiled but didn't answer. And he was still holding my hand. Although my mother had already told me a little about him, I asked, "How did you end up in Dalton Springs?"

"Aunt Daisy and Uncle Marv wanted to go on this big RV trip, but she didn't want to close the shop. I was working at a nursery in California, and she asked me if I was interested in running things for her. I thought, *What the hell. I need something new.* I came up here for the year, and then I didn't leave." He leaned closer. "My dad served in the Marine Corps. We moved around a lot. My family's great, but I never had a permanent home. When I came here, everyone was so friendly. It was like I'd grown up here just because Crazy Daisy was my aunt. I wanted to stay."

His thumb ran over mine as he went on. "What you said about coming to the café—your Dad and the comic books and now you're here tonight—I've never had anything like that. You asked why I was into plants. Maybe this sounds crazy, but I was always looking for roots. I guess I found them here."

"It doesn't sound crazy."

He told me about starting Soil and Green, the books he liked and the ones he didn't. I told him the entire plot of *Under the Gypsy Moon,* and we laughed at the goofy parts. In fact, we laughed a lot.

It was almost ten when our waitress came over. "Hey, boys, we close in a couple of minutes."

I hadn't realized we'd been there for so long. We paid our tab and left a tip big enough to make her chatter at the man behind the counter.

As we headed toward the inn, I knew *someone* would be waiting up wanting details, so I hoped to make it a long walk.

Eric stopped. "There's something I've always wanted to do. Tonight, I'm going to do it."

He jogged to the fountain and jumped in as I followed and watched.

"This is why I love Dalton Springs, Jimmy. Have you ever been here in the afternoon?" He kicked some water at me. "Everyone stops by. They throw a penny in, and they make a wish. How many wishes do you think this thing holds?" He splashed me again.

I jumped into the water, pulled him to me and gave him a kiss. I didn't have an answer, but I believed there was room for one wish more.

SHEP: A DOG

Alex Jeffers

Black crows on a floating branch. No, that was dumb, crows weren't seabirds. Cormorants? Isaac needed the right line, the right words. The right birds. Poetry sucked.

He looked out over the water again. A gray wall of fog loomed just outside the bay. The waves were pathetic; even he, who had never seriously contemplated mounting a surfboard, could tell. But what he was looking for was Jackson. Jackson, who was out there beyond the lackluster surf line, one of seven figures bobbing on the swell, unfairly identical in black neoprene, waiting for something to happen. Jackson probably had no use for poetry because Jackson was pretty nearly perfect and poetry was for losers like Isaac.

Isaac capped his pen and closed the bound notebook over seventeen failed attempts to write something to make Jackson notice him. The submissions deadline for *The Sand Dollar* was a week away. Not that Jackson would read *The Sand Dollar.* Nobody but proud parents actually read *The Sand Dollar.*

Jackson would read edgy blogs and the surf report. Because Jackson was perfect. Except for barely knowing that Isaac drew breath and for already having a boyfriend.

Who was probably off doing political advocacy or building sets for the spring musical instead of sitting on the beach mooning after somebody else's sweetheart, because Hank was irritatingly perfect, too. He even had the perfect name and most everybody (except Isaac) thought he was marginally cuter than Jackson. They were the perfect couple. Last year's yearbook featured more candid-couple photos of Hankson than Carmel High's (admittedly weak) starting quarterback and his science-fair-winning girlfriend. Isaac's girlfriends sighed over how lovely Hankson were, separately and together. It was sick and twisted of Isaac to want to break them up, kick Hank to the curb and fly off over the rainbow with Jackson.

Who probably had appalling taste in music. All surfers did: reggae, white hip-hop. Maybe even the Beach Boys. Jackson probably wasn't as smart as Isaac wanted him to be, his appearances on the honor roll due to teachers taken in by his beauty and amiability—Hank probably rewrote all his papers for him. He probably never read any book that wasn't assigned. He probably watched only reality TV. He was probably dull and would spend any date they ever went on—an unlikelihood—exchanging texts with his bros. Until they got to the sex part, when he would prove to have a disappointing dick.

Which he would know exactly what to do with to bring Isaac to unspeakable ecstasy, because running Jackson down wasn't working. Isaac adjusted himself in his shorts. He was doomed to a loveless, sexless, Jacksonless future, no companion but a trusty right hand, no matter how many times Meg assured him he was cute as pie and only needed to get out of town to meet boys who'd appreciate him.

"This is stupid," he said aloud. "And humiliating."

"Yes. Precisely."

Isaac's heart banged and his stomach tried to jump up his throat. "Where did you come from?" he yelped.

Looming over Isaac, Meg gave him a witchy smile. "Oh, you know me," she said airily. "Always popping up where I'm least wanted and most needed." Her floaty black skirt, lace-up boots, and biker jacket looked even more out of place on the beach than they did at school. Fiddling with the antique seals and amulets strung on chains around her neck, she gazed at the inhumanly patient surfers on the bay. "You weren't answering my texts so I took a wild guess."

Isaac's heart was still going double time. He didn't believe Meg ever guessed at anything. "Phone's safer locked in the car."

"So would you be."

"What do you want, Meg?"

"Besides a breath of fresh sea air and another chance to watch my bestie act like a lovelorn idiot?"

She pushed bushy hair out of her eyes and sunlight glanced off her big silver and amethyst pentacle ring right into Isaac's eyes so that he had to blink. For an instant, distorted by tears, Meg looked very strange, kind of scary, not like a high school senior with a halfhearted case of the goths. Isaac rubbed his eyes. When he could see again, Meg was sitting on the sand beside him and didn't look any weirder than usual.

"What do *you* want, Ike?" she asked.

His voice too loud, Isaac said, "Don't call me Ike."

"I mean, obviously, I know what you want that you can't have, and you know I don't approve."

Taking a deep breath, Isaac looked away and counted to five instead of strangling his best friend. The swell didn't appear any more promising. Straddling their boards, the seven surfers were still just sitting there and he still couldn't pick out which one was Jackson.

Meg cleared her throat. "You know, Isaac, there are several other high schools within twenty-five minutes' drive of here. I bet they all have boys. Possibly even gay boys. Maybe, just maybe, cute gay boys who like poetry. *Single* boys."

"Whether you approve or not doesn't enter the equation, Margaret."

"How's that poem coming?" Meg said sweetly. "I've got pages to fill."

"How 'bout you ask Hank."

"Hank already submitted. A sonnet."

Appalled, Isaac just stared at *The Sand Dollar's* literary editor.

Meg smiled. "Technically proficient—scans right, rhymes in the right places. Too goopy for my taste, but I haven't turned it down yet. I bet his boyfriend loved it."

Isaac's tongue swelled and tasted like poison. Instead of spitting, he said, "That's a deeply unkind thing to say."

Unconcerned, Meg said, "You know, Pre-Raphaelite longing for an inappropriate, inaccessible beloved is out of date and clichéd. Poets don't have to be tortured." Another flash of light from one of her jewels blinded Isaac again. "There's a whole world of boys out there who'd just eat you up. It's unkind of you to fixate on the one who doesn't want you, Ike."

"Don't call me Ike."

"What a pretty dog. Is that a *wave?*"

Scowling, Isaac looked up. The black and white dog had appeared out of nowhere, racing south along the foaming edge of a retreating wave, chasing a yellow tennis ball that threw up spray in its wake without ever slowing. Isaac thought that might violate the laws of physics but he didn't care about dogs—Lily, his cat back at home, made sure of that.

Rushing out, the wash collided with a low-breaking comber, another behind it slightly higher. Amusing for little kids with Styrofoam boogie boards, maybe. Farther out, a tall hump of swell bellied over the kelp beds toward land. Isaac had watched Jackson surf often enough to believe it had potential, but where *was* Jackson? Where were the other six surfers? Isaac shot to his feet.

The hump rose, took on definition, towered. Just as froth began to boil along the crest, one and then another sharp-beaked cormorant broke the glassy blue-green wall, black wings frantic. A moment later, four more followed in a rush, clearing the tube as it formed and began to topple.

"What?" shouted Isaac. "Where's Jackson?"

As if its name were called, a final cormorant burst through the foaming crest. A silver fish too big to swallow all at once wriggled in its beak as it swooped toward shore, the wave collapsing mightily behind it.

"Jackson?"

Delighted, the dog Isaac had forgotten veered away from the yellow ball, yapping, galloping after the skimming black bird into hock-deep wash, oblivious of the crashing confusion of a broken comber rushing at it and the taller wave following. A scornful cormorant lured the dog deeper and then darted into the air as tumbling waters knocked the dog's feet from under it and the larger wave fell.

Isaac ran unthinking. Before he leapt the flotsam-jetsam tide line onto damp sand, the dog got its head above water for a moment but couldn't seem to find its feet in the battling currents. Another wave broke on its head. Isaac was knee-deep in the chilly surf—then crotch deep when the next collapsing swell caught him, nearly taking his feet with it. He found the struggling dog, muzzle high, trying to float, trying to paddle, and managed to get one arm under its chest, lifting it against his own chest.

The dog went limp. Adjusting his hold to support the hindquarters, Isaac turned to carry it back to dry land. A last malicious wave smacked his ass and then he was free, staggering through shin-high retreating wash. At least the dog wasn't as heavy as he'd expected.

He glanced back over his shoulder. The bay had resumed its near calm, troubled only by a low swell that barely broke before it hit sand and hissed a few yards inland. The fog bank had advanced. No sign of bobbing surfers straddling their boards—or bobbing surferless boards. That was somehow a relief.

Isaac waited till the sand clogging his feet was dry, beyond the fringe of stinking kelp, before he set his soggy burden down on its own feet. He was soggy, too: squelchy sneakers, wet jeans, wet halfway up his sweater and the Red Caps T-shirt underneath. The dog just stood there, head low, its panting mixed with coughs, but at least it didn't fall over.

"Doggy?" said Isaac. "Are you all right?"

After a moment, the dog turned its head toward him.

"Where's your owner, doggy?"

The dog sneezed and looked up again with a panting grin.

"It's technically illegal for you to be on the beach off leash."

Lowering its head again, the dog shook enthusiastically. Dog-scented spray showered Isaac, soaking him where he wasn't already wet. Long, thick fur held *a lot* of seawater.

"Of course you would, doggy," Isaac said, resigned. "Of course I didn't bring a towel because nobody but crazed surfers in wetsuits ever go into Carmel Bay, because it's really freaking cold. Are you feeling better? Where's your owner? Find your owner, boy. Girl. Whatever you are."

The dog just stared doggily into his eyes.

"I'm not a dog person. I mean, I don't dislike dogs but I don't have a lot of experience. I rescued you, isn't that enough? Go find your owner."

The dog's wet tail waved. Black feathers clumped by damp reminded Isaac irresistibly of long eyelashes, tear clumped—a boy's thick lashes, if any boy ever came close enough, if Isaac were worth crying over. Taking two steps toward him, the dog sat, tail brushing the sand. Adoring eyes the color of fresh caramel tried to melt Isaac.

"That's not fair, doggy. I don't know you. Where's your owner?" Although Isaac knew almost nothing about dogs, he'd seen *Babe* at an impressionable age so he was pretty sure this one, with its white muzzle and forehead blaze, white chest and front legs, was a border collie. "You're supposed to be so smart—*find your owner.*"

Looking up and down the length of the beach, Isaac was peculiarly unsurprised to see no people at all. Even Meg had vanished from beside his knapsack up the sandy slope. The abandonment smarted: Meg had pointed out the dog. Isaac turned to check the water. Still no surfers on the rocking bay about to be consumed by fog. No other dogs on the sand or frolicking at the Pacific's fringes—no physics-defying neon tennis ball. Gulls in the air, and prancing about at the waterline, seven cormorants bobbing on the swell beyond the low, tireless surf. The breeze off the bay chilled him where he was wet. Almost all of him. He started to shiver.

"I have to—" Isaac looked at the dog. Head cocked to the side, it looked back at him, floppy leaf-shaped black ears half pricked, eyes friendly. "I rescued you and I'm not sorry, but my responsibility ended there. Find your owner. I have to get home, get dry and warm." He strode right past the dog onto drier, deeper sand that tested his ankles.

His notebook lay half buried beside the knapsack. Shaking sand from the pages, Isaac reflected that at least the dog had gotten his mind off mooning after Jackson. Maybe he could write a sonnet about saving a dog lost in the surf? No. A lost and struggling boy. And not a sonnet, not if Hank had written one for *The Sand Dollar.* Something tougher. A sestina? As he scanned about for his pen, he noticed with a mild thrill of unease that there was no evidence of Meg—no depression in the sand where she'd been sitting, no prints from her Doc Martens coming or going.

The pen was not to be found either. Cheap Pilot; didn't matter. He stuffed the book into the knapsack's open pocket. Appearing from nowhere, the dog nosed at the pack, barked questioningly when Isaac lifted it out of reach.

"No! Bad dog."

Sitting, alert, the dog barked again.

"I don't know you," Isaac said, irritated. "Go away. Find your owner." Irritated with the dog, with its negligent owner, with himself for being irritated. The animal didn't understand English. Throwing the knapsack onto his shoulder, Isaac started up the hill toward the Eighth Avenue stairs.

The dog followed him, of course. Followed halfway to the stairs, then loped around and ahead. At one of the sandstone boulders concreted into the stairs' foundation below the ice-plant-burdened retaining wall, it paused, grinned back at him, and lifted its leg. A boy dog, then. *His* leg.

Giving up, Isaac sighed and sat on the lowest redwood step. "Why won't you leave me alone, doggy?" The dog pushed between his thighs, absurdly happy to be acknowledged. "Why won't you go back to your owner? Or your house—do you belong nearby? Did you get loose and run away to the beach?" Gingerly, Isaac scratched at the soft, damply sticky fur between its ears. The dog wriggled with joy.

"Do you even have an owner? Do you have a collar, boy? Tags?"

Probing the thick ruff, he found slimy leather, rotated it through his fingers past the buckle to the leash loop. One tag. As Isaac leaned to inspect it, the dog licked his cheek, panted wetly in his ear. "Stop that." One tag that wasn't a county dog license. "So you're not just illegally off leash on the beach, you're illegal in general. Bad dog." Isaac's heart wasn't in it. The dog licked him again.

The name SHEP was engraved on the brass tag. But no phone number, just a street address in Pacific Grove. Six-plus miles over the hill via 68, the shortest driving route—a whole lot farther around the Peninsula, whether by road or cove to cove and trespassing across all the golf courses. "How'd you get all the way to Carmel, Shep boy? Bad dog."

Hearing his name, Shep yapped right in Isaac's ear. Isaac pushed him away. "Hey, now. There are *standards* in polite society. No deafening the person who saved your life."

Shep lowered his head as if ashamed, then crowded back against Isaac's leg.

"Okay, I'm sorry." Isaac scratched behind Shep's ear. "We have to think now. I don't have a clue where Lobos Ave is in PG but I guess that's what GPS is for."

Pounding inland without warning, a gust of chilly wind made him shiver again. Unthinking, he buried his face in the ruff of Shep's neck. Damp, sticky, salty, it wasn't much comfort.

"I'm sorry, Shep," Isaac muttered. "I need a hot shower and dry clothes before anything else. Your careless owners will just have to wait another hour."

Pulling himself to his feet, Isaac started up the steps. Scampering claws on redwood didn't follow him. He looked back. At the foot of the stairs, Shep stared up at him sadly. "Oh, come on.

I'm taking responsibility for you, all right? I'll make sure you get home to Lobos Avenue."

The dog shook his head as if Isaac was talking nonsense.

"Shep!"

The dog's ears rose.

"Here, boy. No more shenanigans."

With a bark of joy, Shep catapulted up the stairs, right past Isaac, who shook his head in sorrow and yelled, "I said no shenanigans! Watch for traffic!"

Shep danced on the tarmac for Isaac when he reached the lay-by at the foot of Eighth. It relieved Isaac to see all the cars parked under the cypresses along the ocean side of Scenic, if still no people, and no cars creeping up behind him from downtown. Just as well with Shep off leash. Still, on impulse, Isaac said, "Shep, heel!" and the good dog fell into step behind him as he started along the street to his own car.

A battered seven-year-old Nissan, it looked forlorn under the glowering windows of multimillion-dollar Scenic Road houses. Isaac peered in the rear window before opening the door: his old saffron-yellow hoodie, the color of which now made him cringe—nothing to be ruined by having a wet, sandy dog sit on it except the seat itself. "In you get, Shep boy."

Hopping in agreeably, Shep scrambled to the back and sat up neatly, panting and grinning.

Isaac got in the front. When he turned the key, the Red Caps album in the CD player started up mid-song, but it didn't seem to bother Shep so Isaac left it running while he fiddled with the heat. No fan till it warmed up. Waiting, he unlocked the glove box, pulled out his phone. Messages—texts: *Meg. Meg. Meg.* One of them had better be an apology for vanishing on him while he was being heroic. Whatever. She could wait till Isaac completed his errand of mercy. Tossing the phone on the passenger seat, he strapped himself in, checked on Shep in the rearview mirror and thought to power the dog's window down six inches. Dogs liked wind in their faces. Not Isaac, whose shivers had barely abated. "Off we go," he said.

At Thirteenth, a car clearly from out of town waited too long at the stop sign, confused by the principle of right of way. After the appropriate moments, Isaac drove through his own stop sign with a wave, obscurely relieved by evidence that everybody everywhere hadn't been Raptured while he was busy with Shep.

More cars on Santa Lucia. Up and over the hill, down past the Mission, into the Fields. Isaac turned left, left again onto his street. No cars in the drive. His mom and dad wouldn't be back from the gallery for hours and big sister Caro was probably doing something extracurricularly creditable for her transfer application from community college to Berkeley. When Isaac pulled in, Shep yapped questioningly.

"No, it's not your house. It's my house. I told you, I need a shower and dry clothes."

Shep was curious when he got out of the car, nosing along the edge of the lawn, but followed Isaac around the side of the house to the back gate. On the deck, Isaac looked at the dog wagging his tail, at the door, around the yard. As far as he knew, there hadn't been another dog in his yard in the twenty years since his parents bought the house: it would be criminally boring for Shep. Who was still damp, and sticky with salt.

"You want a bath, Shep?" Isaac didn't have dog shampoo but boy shampoo couldn't hurt. It wasn't like Isaac bought Axe. "Come along." Before he opened the door, he remembered Lily and bent to grab Shep's collar, muttering, "You *will not* chase my cat."

Just in time. Glowering, Lily sat in the doorway between kitchen and living room. Shep made a strangled noise but didn't struggle. Nevertheless, Lily spat and fled. Still holding on, Isaac led the dog the other way, to the bathroom between his room and Caro's.

Washing a dog was far less traumatic than the one time Isaac had tried to bathe Lily, though Shep had at least thirty pounds on her. He seemed to enjoy it. It took six bath towels to get him back to acceptably damp, though, and Isaac eyed Caro's blow-dryer speculatively for a moment. He was sodden himself, hands and arms cruddy with long black and white hairs. Sitting on the floor, he hugged the towel-wrapped dog for a long time. Shep smelled like pomegranates. Lily might have purred, if Lily put up with hugs. "You're more comforting than my cat, Shep," he murmured, feeling disloyal, and Shep licked his ear.

Isaac decided not to risk leaving Shep alone in his room. Too many things for a curious wet dog to get into, too much cat smell—sleeping on his pillow was the acme of Lily's displays of affection—and the latch wasn't trustworthy. Leaving the damp, hairy towels to make a nest, he said, "Lie down, Shep."

Obliging, Shep curled up, looking dramatic against forest-green and dusty-rose terry cloth. Isaac pulled his damp, hairy T-shirt off and unclasped his belt, then glanced at the dog regarding him calmly, steadily. It was stupid, but Isaac turned his back before getting naked. "Just us boys," he muttered, climbing into the tub, praying Shep hadn't used up all the hot water.

He hadn't, but the loose hair he'd left clogged the drain so that scummy water climbed to Isaac's ankles before he was ready to get out from under the shower. The thought that finally moved him was: *What if somebody comes home early?* How would Shep react to people noises outside the locked door? How would people react to Shep? Isaac's dad would be all *How brave of you to plunge into the ocean to rescue an innocent puppy!* but Caro and their mom were weirdly protective of bad-tempered

Lily's sensibilities. Although Lily was Isaac's cat. He'd named her, he fed her and cleaned her litter box.

Shep raised his head with a grin when Isaac emerged from behind the shower curtain. The way the dog looked at him made Isaac stupidly self-conscious. He dried off fast—it was great to be warm again—wrapped his own towel around his waist, grabbed Shep by the collar and stuck his head out the door. Lily was lurking in the hall. She glared until Shep's head came out at knee height, then dashed away. "See?" said Isaac. "You'd better have owners because there's no way you could ever live here." Then, feeling anticipatorily wistful, "I hope they'll let me visit you."

He brought Shep into his bedroom, dressed quickly, then left him with a stern, "Three minutes—no mischief," to extract the plug of dog hair from the bathtub drain and throw the towels in the washing machine.

No mischief. Shep hadn't even climbed onto the bed. "Who's a good boy? If I had a Milk-Bone it'd be yours right now." Gazing at Shep, sitting neatly, patiently, eyes shining, Isaac thought, *I really want to keep you. What kind of cat guy does that make me?* "Let's get out of here. Have to get you home. Heel, Shep. No chasing the cat."

Shep at his heel, he opened the door. Lily had apparently learned her lesson and was nowhere to be seen. Shep followed him obediently through the house, the yard, to the car. He hopped in, maybe a little less eagerly than the first time. Isaac leaned in to ruffle his ears before closing the door. "You're going home, boy," he said, wondering if that was really a good thing. What kind of owners let their dog loose on the streets?

In the driver's seat, he took two minutes to program Shep's address into the GPS app of his phone, ignored yet another text from Meg, and then turned it off before it could start giving him directions to the highway. Seventeen minutes later, at a red light on the edge of built-up Pacific Grove, he turned it on again, followed its peremptory turn-by-turns until he reached a pleasant-looking bungalow with a gabled dormer window above the wide, shadowy front porch. There was plenty of room at the curb, no need for fancy parallel parking or the rearview mirror. Parked, engine off, he said, "Shep?"

From the backseat, an unmistakably human voice said, "Umm. Yeah?"

The shoulder belt tried to kill Isaac when he whipped around and craned to look between the seats. "What?" he yelped.

The boy in Isaac's backseat said uncertainly, "Shep. That's my name." The cute boy in cute glasses and nothing else except a leather cord and a house key around his neck. He seemed to realize he was nude in the same instant as Isaac and moved his hands to cover his crotch.

"You—"

"Breathe. Listen. Yes, *I know.* I was a dog a minute ago. Weird, huh? So weird let's neither of us think about it." His voice made Isaac tingle. He offered a smile that was half apology, half gratitude. "So as long as I'm in your car and you know my name, what's yours?"

"Uh—"

"No, really."

"Isaac." Isaac swallowed. Boy Shep was *extremely* cute, his thick black hair tousled into tufts and his caramel-colored eyes magnified by the spectacles. "Look, is that actually your house? Because you're, uh, naked in my car on a public street."

"I am, aren't I?" Shep glanced out the window. "Yeah, that's it. But the parents are out of town this week and I'm, like, lacking pockets, so no key."

"Around your neck."

Raising his eyebrows above the frames of his glasses, Shep

lifted one hand to his chest. Nice chest. A little sprinkle of hair down the middle. "Huh," he said. "Whoever turned me into a dog was thinking ahead."

"It had your address on it when it was a tag on your collar. And your name."

Shep shrugged. "I'm still stark naked and I have to say the thought of streaking across my front yard and fumbling with the lock in broad daylight doesn't fill me with joy."

Isaac blinked, thinking he wouldn't mind if Shep never put on clothes again. But that was unreasonable. "It's ugly," he said, nodding at the puddle of yellow hoodie on the seat next to Shep, "but you could cover the strategic bits with that. Until you get inside."

"I guess. Huh—oh, wait. You're coming with me."

"I am?"

Shep nodded vigorously. "Don't even think about driving away."

Intensely relieved, Isaac nodded back. "You wanna? I'll check if there's people gawking."

"Not really, but I guess."

Pulling the keys from the ignition and grabbing his phone, Isaac got out. He looked up and down the street, at the houses on either side. He stuck his head back in, said, "Coast looks clear."

Wearing the hoodie like a saffron-colored diaper, Shep hopped out of the car and dashed up the path and the porch stairs. Shadow hardly obscured his bare back and brilliant yellow ass while he unlocked the front door. Isaac realized he was short—not dwarfish, but shorter than him. He'd always liked tall guys before, but tall guys weren't Shep. Isaac beeped the car doors locked and followed. Shep was already inside, poking his head around the open door. "Come on, Isaac!"

"Sorry," Isaac began to say, but Shep slammed the door.

"Naked here," he blurted, scampering away. The sweatshirt diaper fell off. "Need clothes."

No, you don't, Isaac wanted to say, watching Shep's cute butt vanish around a corner. *Just us boys. No big. No homo.* He plucked up the yellow hoodie and started after. *No—plenty of homo. I could take mine off, too.*

Around the corner, three doors off the short hallway were closed. "Shep?" Isaac called.

"Upstairs."

The voice came down around another corner. Isaac hadn't noticed the stairs that started under the stained-glass window at the end of the hall. He climbed halfway, paused when he saw the poster on the landing wall where the stairs took a right angle. It had a LOLdog caption but he didn't read it: the border collie running down a beach looked so much like the dog Shep had been that he choked. Anxious, he clattered up the last few steps, burst through the open door.

In the center of the attic bedroom, still a boy, Shep was half into a T-shirt. When he pulled it down, the neckband dislodged his glasses and he had to grab for them before they fell out the bottom. The three inches of his boxers exposed by unbelted jeans had a print of gamboling puppies—Isaac couldn't be sure they were border collies. Before he put the glasses back on, Shep looked up and grinned. "Hey." His brown eyes were just as pretty naked. Thick black lashes. "Now I'm at less of a disadvantage."

Isaac tried to smile back. Before he knew what was happening, Shep was right up close. He grabbed both Isaac's arms, went up on tiptoes and kissed him.

Scared out of his wits, Isaac kissed him back. It went on a long time. He needed a place to put his hands, which turned out to be Shep's butt. Without his actually thinking about it, his fingertips dug in. It felt really good, but not as good as kissing and being kissed.

Gasping, Shep broke off for a breath but didn't let Isaac go. He said, "Oh, good, you *are* gay."

"Uh, yeah?"

"You don't have a boyfriend already, do you? I don't want to step on any toes."

Shep, Isaac discovered, was standing barefoot on the toes of *his* sneakers. He inhaled. "There's a guy—" Jackson. Jackson the surfer. Who he'd forgotten all about until now and who was taken, and if surreally handsome, wasn't as real as this boy. "No. No, there isn't. No, I don't." Holding on to Shep's butt, he pulled the real boy closer. "I'd like to, though."

"Me, too," Shep said, and kissed him again.

That went on, deliciously, until the phone in Isaac's pocket trilled. Shep said into his open mouth, "Maybe you should get that."

"It's just a text. Just Meg."

"Meg?" Not letting go, Shep leaned back to look into Isaac's eyes. "Meg Stornoway?"

"You know Meg?"

"I'm the editor of PG High's annual lit 'zine, she edits your school's, so yeah. I think I might be pissed at her now, though, for never introducing me to you."

"Uh," said Isaac as an extremely peculiar feeling rippled down his spine. Without allowing Shep to fall, he fumbled the phone out one-handed, thumbed at icons on the screen. *So,* the newest Meg text read, *is Shep a good kisser?* Showing it to Shep, Isaac said, "That bitch. That *witch*. She turned you into a dog."

"Do you wish she hadn't?" Shep asked.

Isaac didn't have an answer so he kissed the adorable boy hanging on to his shoulders. First time he'd initiated one. He might be getting the hang of it. When they were both breathless again, he gasped, "Do you?"

"I—" Hugging him harder, Shep laid his head on Isaac's shoulder. "I liked it. I didn't *understand* it, because I was a dog, and it was really frustrating when you started talking to me and I didn't know what the words meant. But I liked it. But I don't want to do it again. I want to be me, a boy, with a—with an incredibly cute potential boyfriend who saved my life." His hand gripped Isaac's ass almost painfully. "That's you, you know. Saved my life and gave me a bath."

"I'm not cute."

Shep let go abruptly, took a step back, looking fierce behind his glasses. "A lot you know, Isaac Whatever-your-last-name-is. Your *nose* is cute. Your *eyes* are cute. Your lips and five-o'clock shadow and freckles are cute. Your ginger hair. You being just the right bit taller than me is *adorable.* You taking care of me when I was a dumb animal was beyond cute."

Isaac gulped. "You're the cute one, Shep. My last name is Hadley."

Shep snorted. "Mine's Power. What're you gonna tell Meg?"

Isaac looked at the phone still in his hand. He thumbed icons, then the keyboard. *The. Best,* he typed, and showed it to Shep before hitting SEND. "I don't have much experience, Shep Power, but I stand by that."

"We can practice more if you like," said Shep.

Isaac felt his face go hot.

"Your blushes are cute!" crowed Shep.

"Umm," said Isaac, cheeks getting hotter. Then he leaned forward to kiss Shep again. Who still smelled like pomegranate shampoo and maybe a little bit like wet dog.

THERE'S NO QUESTION IT'S LOVE

N. S. Beranek

The old well is located in an odd place. Near the front corner of our lawn, it's just far enough away from both the street and the driveway to make converting its waist-high bricks into a mailbox holder a pointless endeavor. You'd have to tromp over too much grass to reach it for that to be viable in this place, where it rains more days than it's dry.

When I reach him, Bob is leaning over the curving brick, holding a penny between his thumb and forefinger. It's clear he's about to drop it through one of the squares in the section of rabbit-wire fencing that we put over the well's opening to keep small children and animals from falling down it.

Though it's obvious what he's doing, I feel compelled to ask. "Making a wish?"

"No."

It takes me a few seconds to process that he's replied negatively. "No?"

"No."

Okaaaaay, I think. "Then what are you doing?"

He shrugs. "I don't know." He exhales deeply, the sound of a man who feels the weight of the world bearing down on him. "Conditioning myself, I suppose."

"To what?"

"To having nothing happen." Hand still poised over the opening, he turns and locks eyes with me. His irises are so dark I'd swear he doesn't have pupils. "Listen," he commands. He lets the coin drop.

I hear nothing, as if the penny is still falling, soaring through an endless space, although when we bought the house, the inspector said the well had been closed up years before, most likely because it ran dry. I can't remember how far he said it was down to the blockage, a mass of construction debris and dirt. A hundred feet? Fifty?

Finally I ask, "Did you hear it?"

"No. That's the point." Bob reaches into his jeans pocket and pulls out a handful of change. He chooses a quarter and tosses it through the grate. We listen again. There is still nothing. No sound. He returns the change to his pocket and for a second I think that he's done, but then his arm juts out and I see he's dangling his car keys and door-lock remote over the hole. Without stopping to think I grab the sleeve of his denim jacket and pull his arm back.

"Are you out of your mind?" I ask as I wrench the keys from his grip. "Do you know how expensive it would be to replace these?"

He just looks at me.

"You're going to throw your keys down the well—why?" I ask.

"They're bigger." He thinks another moment. "Though that won't change anything."

"And this is to condition yourself to having nothing happen?" I'm openly mocking him now, not even trying to hide my derision. Bob nods. I have the urge to put a hand to my head and tug my hair in frustration. Instead I say, "Pray tell, what does that mean?"

He shrugs again.

"Well, then can you at least tell me if you're aware that you sound like a madman?" It occurs to me right then that I'm cringing, though it's not because of anything he's done; he may not be self-aware at this moment, but I've just heard myself peppering him with questions. I hate the way I speak, always either asking questions or making statements that I then turn into questions by raising my pitch at the end of the sentence. It's something I can't keep from doing; no matter how I intend my phrases when I begin them, they always get distorted this way.

You talk like a girl, my older brother Ron would accuse when we were kids. I know exactly where he got it, a favorite piece of advice from our maternal grandfather: *A man should say only what he means, and own what he says.*

My sudden realization about what's really going on with Bob stops me from spiraling off into a prolonged self-pity session inspired by my imperfect childhood.

"Wait, is this about the story?" I ask. His silence and turning away assure me that I'm right. I roll my eyes at his back. It's only been a week and a half since he sent his story to a magazine he found listed on a fiction-markets website. He can't really be upset that he hasn't gotten a reply, can he?

I tell myself this is nothing but a cry for attention. Self-pity, indeed. But a moment later I feel the twinge; he's sad and scared. I have to fix it.

He's striding away from me, already halfway across the grass, making a beeline for the porch. I have to jog to catch up with him. "Didn't they say it would take ninety days at least?"

"I'm not talking about the magazine."

You're not talking about anything, I think. "Then what?"

"I sent it to Frannie yesterday," he says, shouldering open the door. He steps inside and begins pulling off his jacket. "Yesterday, and I still haven't heard back. Nothing. Not even to say she got it."

Frannie used to be our across-the-way neighbor, but three years ago she and her husband Walt moved to the other big city in our state in order to be closer to their grown kids, who both settled there after college. This weekend they're back for a rare visit. Last night we all went to dinner. When Frannie—an English lit major in college and a voracious reader to this day—heard that Bob's skin had finally thickened enough to allow him to begin sending his stories out, to risk hearing someone's opinion besides mine, she graciously offered to give him feedback.

I feel awful for not realizing that's what has made him such a basket case. We've been together for fifteen years and lived together for almost that long. More than anyone, I know how raw he is where his writing is concerned. Plus I felt his energy rise last night when she made the offer. It would've been impossible not to feel it. Probably folks on the International Space Station felt it.

He drops his car keys in the square mahogany bowl on the hall table and picks up the three new pieces of junk mail I set there earlier.

Intending to inject a little levity into the moment, I force a laugh. "How do you figure that was yesterday?" He'd emailed his story to Frannie not ten minutes after we got home the night before, which was well after midnight.

"It's yesterday before you go to sleep. Once you wake up it's today," Bob declares. He tosses the junk mail into the wicker trash receptacle under the hall table. Like the bowl and half the other furnishings in our home, it is made of dark-hued, natural materials. Our kitchen counters and bathroom vanities are black granite; the flooring throughout the house is walnut-stained bamboo; the rugs are wool woven in bold geometric, earth-toned designs.

I step behind him, slide my arms around his waist and hug him tight. "Mmm. Is that how that works?" He smells fantastic, a mix of laundry dried on the line, fresh-brewed coffee and love. I want to hold on to him this way forever.

"Frannie's always been an early riser," he reasons. "You know that. She probably got it five hours ago."

"Yes, and they have a whole agenda planned for this trip, remember? So many things they wanted to do that they had no choice but to pass on some of them?" I hug him harder. When I relax, I feel him do the same. I kiss his shoulder. "Why don't you go upstairs and try to write something new?"

"That's a good idea." He twists around to face me. We kiss, and he tastes even better than he smells. I move my hands to the sides of his face in an attempt to keep him where he is. Too soon, and despite my efforts, he wriggles free. "If we keep that up," he chides, "I won't get any writing done today."

I arch a brow. "Would that be so bad?"

It's his turn to laugh. "I can't answer that!" He leans close again, this time pressing his forehead to mine. "You always make me feel better," he says. "Thank you."

I feel myself blush. "How about Mexican for lunch? Do tacos sound good? Or burritos?"

He screws up his lips as he considers it. "Enchiladas."

"Beef or chicken?"

"Whatever." He straightens up again, slips from my grasp and heads for the stairs.

"Promise," I call after him, "you won't check your email obsessively?"

SAVE THE LAST DANCE FOR ME

David Puterbaugh

We're watching my boyfriend dance.

Gene and Ed are drinking scotch, and I'm nursing a vodka tonic. Matthew's martini waits for him at his place at our table.

This is not a cruise that Matthew and I are on with Gene and Ed, but a transatlantic crossing. Seven days at sea from England to New York, just like the sailings of years past before jet travel, when the rich and famous crossed the Atlantic in glamorous black and white. "Fodor's calls it the most regal ship to cross the Atlantic in this or any era," Gene emailed us six months ago when we made our reservations. "We'll be the Queens of the World!"

The dance floor is wide—"the largest dance floor at sea," we learned on a ship tour after our departure from Southampton five days ago—and there are crystal chandeliers hanging above it from the ballroom's high ceiling. At the front of the ballroom is the grand staircase, where Gene insisted we pose tonight for a photo after dinner. Gene never misses an opportunity for a camera. His impression of Shelley Winters in *The Poseidon Adventure* is spot-on. ("In the water I'm a very skinny lady!")

This evening is our last formal night before our arrival in New York, and the ship's daily program politely suggested black tie for tonight's festivities. Many of the ladies in the room are wearing cocktail dresses and ball gowns. And like most of the men on board our foursome is wearing tuxedos. On the stage beside the grand staircase a band is playing Gershwin's "The Man I Love," and Ed is humming along.

My boyfriend and I are two of the youngest passengers on board. Matthew is thirty-nine, and I turned forty last month. If I had to guess I'd say the average age of the ship's passengers is sixty-five. Gene and Ed are both seventy, but I never think of them as senior citizens. "Whatever you do, don't stand behind an old person in line," Gene instructed us one afternoon at the lunch buffet. "If they have a heart attack you could miss the desserts."

Gene points to the dance floor as Matthew comes gliding by with one of our tablemates from dinner, a divorced real estate agent from Houston named Laurel. "Would you look at him out there," Gene says. "That boy really should be on 'Dancing with the Stars.'"

Matthew first learned to dance from his mother, who taught him how to waltz when he was five years old. Now, more than halfway to New York, my boyfriend has developed quite a following. This morning at breakfast two ladies old enough to be our grandmothers stopped Matthew on our way into the restaurant. "You're the young man from the ballroom, aren't you? We love watching you dance."

Matt and I went up to the ship's nightclub our second night on board. The crowd was younger—fiftysomethings—and a DJ was playing Eighties music. There were a couple of dozen people on the dance floor, and when Erasure's "A Little Respect" came on, Matt pulled me up and I went. Dancing in a crowd in the nightclub, I felt we were safe enough.

Matthew keeps telling me to relax. Our cabin attendant, a woman from Peru named Faviola, calls us "mis favoritos" and leaves towel animals for us when she turns down our room. Last night we found two towel swans sitting on our bed. The swans were facing each other with their heads pointed down and their beaks and bodies touching. In the space between their long necks Faviola had created a perfect heart.

Of course some of the ship's crew are gay. Gene giddily points it out whenever he sees a waiter or bartender give me or Matthew "the eye." But many of the passengers don't see us, like the two ladies who stopped us at breakfast. Their generation gave them few words for Matthew and me, for who we are and what we are to each other. One of the ladies asked us if Ed and Gene are our fathers.

I smile at Gene but the truth is I've stopped watching Matthew dance, and I'm now looking at a boy sitting across from us on the other side of the dance floor. He's thirteen or fourteen years old I'm guessing, by far the youngest person on the ship. He is sitting with a man and woman I assume are his parents; they're not much older than Matthew and me. I'm watching this boy as he watches Matthew dance, watching as he brushes his mother off when she appears to ask him to dance with her. I'm watching this boy's eyes follow my boyfriend around the dance floor.

The song ends and we join in as the couples on the dance floor clap for the band. Matthew kisses Laurel's hand and escorts her back to her table, where her friend Diane is drinking champagne. Diane is also from Houston, and like Laurel is divorced and in her midfifties. Our first night onboard, Gene and Diane became fast friends at dinner. Diane's laugh is high and exaggerated like a cartoon character's. Her laugh could be heard throughout the restaurant every time Gene opened his mouth.

Laurel takes her seat and Matthew starts back to our table just as the band begins playing Glenn Miller's "Moonlight Serenade." Diane stands and catches Matthew's arm. It's her turn to dance with my boyfriend.

"It's like watching a dance marathon," Ed says. "But with just one contestant."

"He better not break a heel," Gene says. "They shoot horses at sea, don't they?"

Gene and Ed have both had long careers on Broadway, working behind the scenes with costumes and lighting on many famous productions. Their apartment in Greenwich Village resembles a small Broadway museum. I've known them for years, since the summer of 2003 when I turned thirty. I joined a gay bowling league in Chelsea, where Gene was our captain. Most seasons our team was tied for last place. We called ourselves the Toilet Bowlers.

Two years ago, Gene and Ed semiretired to Fort Lauderdale. Matthew and I spent last New Year's with them at their new condo. As long as I've known Gene he's always had a tan, even in New York in February. If Gene is South Beach, then Ed is New England, specifically a small New England college town in autumn. He reminds me of my favorite English professor.

I turn back to the boy, who's still watching Matthew dance. He's looking at Matthew the way I looked at him the night we met three years ago, when I saw him dancing shoeless at my cousin Steven's wedding. Matthew worked with my cousin's new bride and was seated at a table with a group from their office. When the wedding DJ opened the dance floor I watched him join a bunch of girls from his table in kicking off their shoes. Matt is six-feet-two, but when he's dancing his height never gets in the way. Matthew doesn't move in time with the music but one step ahead, as if his body knows where the rhythm is going even before the lyrics. Like the boy, I couldn't take my eyes off him that night. I never knew gold-toed black socks could be so sexy.

Last night, well past midnight, after Gene and Ed had gone to bed, Matthew and I climbed carpeted steps to the upper decks. Even in June the Atlantic can be too choppy for the heartiest sailor, and outside we had the promenade deck to ourselves. The air blowing up from the sea was cool but we still had our dinner jackets. Matt reached for my hand just as mine went for his.

Matthew walked up to the railing and looked out at the ocean, so dark and mysterious, reflecting stars I've never seen so bright. I stepped up behind him and wrapped my arms around his waist. I could feel the soft vibration beneath my shoes as the ship carried our love to America, steady and onward, like a future that couldn't be stopped. My boyfriend's scent mixed with the salt air as he turned his head back to me and we kissed. In that moment I cared about nothing else but him.

I look at the boy now and I know what he is thinking. I wish I were dancing with Matthew, too.

The song ends and we clap again, and the bandleader announces a short break. Matthew escorts Diane to her seat and returns to our table.

"You have an admirer," Gene says as Matthew takes his seat beside me. I'm only mildly surprised that Gene, too, has noticed the boy.

"Oh, Charlie," Matthew says, following Gene's gaze.

"Charlie?" I say. "You've met him?"

Matthew nods after sipping his martini. "Out by the pool this afternoon, when you went back to the cabin for a nap."

Ed peers across the dance floor. "Is he British?"

Matt nods again. "From London. I think he said his father works for a bank in New York, and his mother is teaching a course on British politics at Columbia this fall. Or is it the other way around? Anyway, he's very sweet."

"He hasn't taken his eyes off you since we came down from dinner," Gene says. "Little Charlie has a crush, I would say."

"How on earth would you know that just by looking at him?" Ed says.

"Because I don't wear trifocals like you, my love."

"Perhaps the boy just likes to dance."

"Perhaps he does, *with other boys*."

"Really, I don't know why you care."

"I don't! I'm simply pointing out that if the lovely Kate Winslet suddenly appeared on the dance floor topless, with the Heart of the Ocean bouncing between her voluptuous breasts, *that boy* wouldn't notice."

Matthew laughs. "I spoke to him first, actually. His parents left him at the pool to go to a wine tasting. Everyone else was swimming and sunning themselves and Charlie was just sitting on a lounge chair all by himself, drawing in an art book. I asked him what he was working on. He's making a comic book."

"Hear that, Dr. Kinsey?" Ed says to Gene. "Not every artistic boy is gay."

"Oh, Charlie is gay," Matthew says. "His main character is this blue alien guy named Cobalt. He has bulging muscles and wears a tiny red Speedo."

"I bet that's where he keeps his super power," Gene says, then raises his hands to his chest when Ed shoots him a look. "What did I say?"

"Cobalt's sidekick is a shirtless cowboy named Rodeo," Matt says, "and in the story, Cobalt and Rodeo help to save a group of school kids who get trapped in a forest fire. At the end, once the kids are safely back on their school bus, Cobalt and Rodeo share a very passionate victory kiss."

Gene nearly spits his scotch on Ed. "He showed you that?"

Matthew grins. "I skipped ahead a little. But Charlie wasn't ashamed of his story, if that's what you mean."

"They didn't have comic books like that when I was a kid," Ed says.

"No, they did not," Gene agrees. "Honestly, this world is changing so fast. Do you realize that by the time that boy is as old as me and Ed he might have legally married as many men as Elizabeth Taylor?"

"You and Ed can still get married you know," Matthew says. "It's not too late."

"How about it Eddie?" Gene says. "Want to marry me once it's legal in Florida?"

"Well I don't know," Ed says, considering the offer. "How do I know you're not just marrying me for my body?"

"Don't be silly, dear," Gene says. "Everyone will know I'm marrying you for your money."

Gene and Ed have been together for forty-six years, longer than my parents. This is their eighteenth transatlantic crossing. They took their first together before Matthew and I were even born.

Ed turns to Matt and me. "What about you two? Should we clear a date on our calendar any time soon?"

Before I can answer my boyfriend speaks for the both of us. "When the time comes I think we'll probably elope. Dan doesn't like a lot of people looking at him."

"That's not—it's not that," I say.

Matthew comes from a touchy-feely family; their love comes wrapped in a bear hug. Before the lights have gone down at the movies, Matthew's hand is on my knee. It's there, too, whenever we drive together in a car. On our flight from New York to London, Matt fell asleep with his head on my shoulder, but I didn't sleep. I was too busy watching the faces of the passengers who passed us on the way to the bathroom. I try not to worry about what other people think. I've tried harder with Matthew than any other man I've ever been with.

Matthew reaches under the table now and puts his hand on my knee. "I meant our wedding will be private, just the two of us." And with this simple expression of his affection, my boyfriend wins. How can I argue what he's saying isn't true when part of me is glad his hand is under the table where no one can see?

The first time I spent the night at Matthew's place—the same night we got silly over a bottle of cabernet at an Italian restaurant in Hell's Kitchen, where our waiter sent us home with biscotti and called us "gents"—I took his hand as we walked to the subway. Matthew has great hands. They're strong, but not calloused or dry. Smooth, and always warm. Sometimes after a long day Matthew will offer to rub my back. I relax before his hands have even touched me. As we got to the subway entrance and started down the stairs, two guys in their twenties were coming up. One had the collar of his blazer popped up, and the other was wearing a fedora. On the surface they looked like two members of a hip boy band, the kind that makes It Gets Better videos for their young gay fans. I didn't feel at all threatened by them as they passed us. But as we got to the bottom of the stairs and they reached the top, one of them said loud enough for Matthew and me to hear, "Two more faggots giving each other AIDS."

"Why does it always have to be such a big deal?" I say quietly, my eyes on the table. "I'm forty years old and I can't kiss my boyfriend on our vacation without worrying we'll get our heads bashed in. Every time I touch him in public it feels like I'm coming out, over and over and over again. What's the point in getting married if I can't show my husband what he means to me? Why does it always have to be such a big deal?" I repeat.

I look up and see the three of them are staring at me. Our waiter approaches the table but Gene signals for him to wait. No one says anything for a long time, and I think I've ruined the evening. But then Ed speaks.

"Because it is a big deal," he says.

He gestures to the room around us. "Do you know in nineteen sixty-five Gene and I couldn't share a cabin? It was too risky. We had to buy two single cabins and hope no one would notice us sneaking in and out of each other's rooms."

"We were sailing on a different ocean back then," Gene says. "We had to be careful not to scare the fishes."

"Then when we could share a cabin we had to explain why we wanted only one bed," Ed says. "We would come back at night to find the cabin steward had pushed the beds apart.

"This," he says, pointing to the four of us around the table, "is a very big deal."

"You can't let the haters get you down, Danny Boy," Gene says. "If they can't see how beautiful you boys are together, fuck 'em."

I look at Matthew and I could cry. One afternoon last week when we were out shopping for our trip, Matthew took my hand a couple of blocks from our apartment. We turned a corner and I saw a group of guys coming toward us. I can't even remember now how many there were or how old they were. They were a group of guys; that was enough. I pulled my hand away from Matthew's.

The guys walked past and ignored us. None of them said or did anything. When I realized Matthew wasn't next to me

I turned around. He was just standing there on the sidewalk, looking at me like I'd physically attacked him. "Do you know how that makes me feel, when you pull away from me like that?" he said. "Like we're nothing. Like you believe we're nothing."

The band returns and begins to play Frank Sinatra's "All the Way." I glance back across the dance floor and lock eyes with Charlie, who isn't looking at Matthew now but at me.

What are you waiting for, Fred Astaire?

I gulp down the rest of my drink and stand.

"Back to the cabin already?" Matthew asks. "Let me finish my drink first."

I hold out my hand. "May I have this dance?"

Ed gives a gasp of surprise. For once Gene is speechless. I can't read the look on Matthew's face.

"Are you serious?" he says.

"I can't talk to you while we're dancing because I'll be counting the steps in my head," I say. "And you'll have to let me lead."

And then it appears, the face I dream about, the one I'll do anything to keep smiling like it is now.

Matthew takes my hand and stands. I can smell the olives from his martini on his lips as he leans in close. "It's your lucky night, sexy man. When it comes to dancing, I go both ways."

We walk onto the floor and face each other. The room is alive with couples in motion, and an elderly couple shuffles by us like they've been dancing to Ol' Blue Eyes for decades. From the corner of my eye I see that Laurel and Diane have spotted us. I watch them dig in their purses for their camera phones as they realize what we're about to do.

"Hey, look at me," Matthew says, and I do. He picks up my right hand with his left, wraps his right arm around me and puts his hand on my back.

"I've got you," he says.

And then we start to dance, and it's true. Matthew's got me and he gets me and he wants me. We're facing each other like the first time we made love. I lead and he follows, he leads and I follow. Two lovers in perfect step. On the largest dance floor at sea in the arms of the man I love, a band serenades us with Sinatra, and I'm keenly aware for however long it lasts this is one of the greatest moments of my life.

Matthew stops dancing suddenly and holds me tighter. He sees something over my shoulder and I fear the worst. Have we angered our fellow passengers? Does the band refuse to play? Is Julie Our Cruise Director rushing toward us with her arms flailing through the air? *Captain Stubing wants that gay shit stopped now! Now! NOW!*

But when I turn my head I see what Matthew sees, and it makes me hold my boyfriend tighter, too. Gene and Ed have left our table and joined us on the dance floor.

They are dancing.

AFTERWORD

Sometimes when I read a collection of stories or a novel, a song will emerge from my memory to become its theme. With this collection, it was Bruce Cockburn's 1983 "Lovers In a Dangerous Time." I suppose any time feels dangerous when we risk our hearts, as the men in these stories do. But men who love men take on the additional challenge of a world that can be hostile toward them because of who they love.

Urban squatters. Young professionals. Boomerang kids. Writers and actors and students. These characters' times are made more dangerous by the consequences of visibility. By poverty. By alcohol and drugs. By illness and injury and disability. By secrets kept and lies told. But still they fumble toward first love, hope to rekindle lost love, and hold tightly to new and true love. Whether their romances are carried out with grace, wit, tenderness, missteps or anxiety, they dare to love in dangerous times.

To paraphrase poet Theodore Roethke, love isn't love until it's vulnerable. As Timothy and I read, considered and accepted stories for this collection, it was the vulnerability of the characters that most often struck me. No matter what, they open their hearts. And open them again. And again. In doing so, they open mine, and long after I've turned their pages, I find myself wondering, *Will he be okay? Will* they *be okay? Will it all work out?*

I think so. I *know* so. I hope you do, too.

R. D. Cochrane

ABOUT THE AUTHORS

SHAWN ANNISTON has worked with lawyers, gamblers and other odd folk. His first short story was published in *Fool For Love*. He's been rewriting the beginning of a novel for several years.

Born and raised in Chicago, **N. S. BERANEK** worked in professional theater for nineteen years. As part of the tenth annual Saints & Sinners Literary Conference in New Orleans, she read a selection from her story "Thou Shalt Not Lie" from *Saints & Sinners 2013: New Fiction from* the *Festival.*

JAMES BOOTH is a writer and book blogger living in Virginia with numerous cats and his awesome best friend. He has run the young adult book blog Book Chic (bookchicclub.blogspot.com) since 2007 and has been quoted on several book covers.

PAUL BROWNSEY is a former newspaper reporter and former philosophy lecturer at Glasgow University, Scotland. His approximately fifty short stories, most of them gay themed, have been published in the United Kingdom and Europe, as well as in North America in *Chiron Review, Not One of Us, Harrington Gay Men's Fiction Quarterly, Dalhousie Review* and *Antigonish Review.* He lives in Scotland.

ROB BYRNES is the author of *The Night We Met, Trust Fund Boys* and the Lambda Award–winning *When the Stars Come Out.* His mysteries include *Straight Lies, Holy Rollers* and *Strange Bedfellows.* A native of upstate New York, he works in Manhattan and lives outside the city with his partner Brady Allen.

TONY CALVERT (deepfriedtony@gmail.com) is an amateur chef, avid fisherman and lover of folktales. His first short story appeared in *Foolish Hearts: New Gay Fiction.* He is currently working on a novel.

JAMESON CURRIER is the author of the novels *Where the Rainbow Ends, The Wolf at the Door* and *The Third Buddha,* and four collections of short fiction. Currier founded Chelsea Station Editions in the spring of 2010.

LEWIS DESIMONE, author of *Chemistry* and *The Heart's History,* has been published in *Chelsea Station, Best Gay Love Stories: Summer Flings, I Like It Like That* and *My Diva: 65 Gay Men on the Women Who Inspire Them.* He lives in San Francisco and is working on his next novel.

ERIC GOBER (ericgober.com) is the author of the novel *Secrets of the Other Side* (Regal Crest Enterprises). He holds an MFA in creative writing from Wichita State University. He lives in L.A., where he's working on a new novel set amidst California's marriage equality battles.

ALEX JEFFERS (sentenceandparagraph.com) has published six books, most recently the novel *Deprivation; or, Benedetto furioso: an oneiromancy*, and forty-plus works of short fiction, most of them gay, many romantic. Originally from Northern California, he has lived in New England a few too many years.

KEVIN LANGSON is a transient writer of short fiction and film reviews currently based in Austin, Texas. Much of his inspiration comes from traveling to new places. He recently spent a year and a half teaching English in Istanbul and returned with many stories to tell.

GEORGINA LI's short stories can be found in *Best Gay Romance 2010* and *2013, Chroma: A Queer Literary Journal, Clean Sheets, Collective Fallout, Federations, Queer Fish* and *Wilde Stories 2010.*

FELICE PICANO is the author of more than twenty-five books of poetry, fiction, memoirs, nonfiction and plays, including *Tales: From a Distant Planet* and *Art & Sex in Greenwich Village.* Picano also began and operated SeaHorse Press and Gay Presses of New York for fifteen years. Picano teaches at Antioch College, Los Angeles.

DAVID PUTERBAUGH received his MFA in creative writing from Queens College, CUNY. A lifelong New Yorker, his stories have been published in numerous anthologies, including *Best Gay Romance 2010, Fool For Love* and *Foolish Hearts*. Follow him on Twitter @DavidPuterbaugh.

JORDAN TAYLOR is the author of short fiction, nonfiction and poetry published by independent presses in the United States, the United Kingdom and Ireland. By day a dog trainer, photographer and World War One enthusiast, Jordan spends as much time as possible reading books by the currently deceased.

ABOUT THE EDITORS

TIMOTHY J. LAMBERT (timothyjlambert.com) lives in Houston with his dogs Pixie P. Lambert and Penny D. Lambert. With R. D. Cochrane, he edited Cleis Press's anthology *Fool For Love: New Gay Fiction* in 2009 and *Foolish Hearts: New Gay Fiction* in 2013. He selected stories and introduced Cleis Press's *Best Gay Erotica 2007,* edited by Richard Labonté. As part of the writing team Timothy James Beck, he wrote *It Had to Be You, He's the One, I'm Your Man, Someone Like You* (a Lambda Literary Award finalist), and *When You Don't See Me.* He cowrote *The Deal* and *Three Fortunes in One Cookie* with Becky Cochrane. His short stories were anthologized in Alyson's *Best Gay Love Stories 2005* and *Best Gay Love Stories NYC Edition,* as well as Cleis Press's *Foolish Hearts: New Gay Fiction.* He's not in love, so don't forget it.

R. D. COCHRANE (beckycochrane.com) grew up in the South, graduated from the University of Alabama and now lives in Texas with her husband and their two dogs, Margot and Guinness. She was coeditor of *Fool For Love: New Gay Fiction* and *Foolish Hearts: New Gay Fiction,* both with Timothy J. Lambert. She cowrote five novels under the name Timothy James Beck, wrote two novels with Timothy J. Lambert and has authored numerous short stories and two contemporary romances, *A Coventry Christmas* and *A Coventry Wedding*. She currently has two novels in progress.

Men on the Make

Wild Boys
Gay Erotic Fiction
Edited by Richard Labonté

Take a walk on the wild side with these fierce tales of rough trade. Defy the rules and succumb to the charms of hustlers, jocks, kinky tricks, smart-asses, con men, straight guys and gutter punks who give as good as they get.
ISBN 978-1-57344-824-6 $15.95

Sexy Sailors
Gay Erotic Stories
Edited by Neil Plakcy

Award-winning editor Neil Plakcy has collected bold stories of naughty, nautical hunks and wild, stormy sex that are sure to blow your imagination.
ISBN 978-1-57344-822-2 $15.95

Hot Daddies
Gay Erotic Fiction
Edited by Richard Labonté

From burly bears and hunky father figures to dominant leathermen, *Hot Daddies* captures the erotic dynamic between younger and older men: intense connections, consensual submission, and the toughest and tenderest of teaching and learning.
ISBN 978-1-57344-712-6 $14.95

Straight Guys
Gay Erotic Fantasies
Edited by Shane Allison

Gaybie Award-winner Shane Allison shares true and we-wish-they-were-true stories in his bold collection. From a husband on the down low to a muscle-bound footballer, from a special operations airman to a redneck daddy, these men will sweep you off your feet.
ISBN 978-1-57344-816-1 $15.95

Cruising
Gay Erotic Stories
Edited by Shane Allison

Homemade glory holes in a stall wall, steamy shower trysts, truck stop rendezvous...According to Shane Allison, "There's nothing that gets the adrenaline flowing and the muscle throbbing like public sex."
ISBN 978-1-57344-795-7 $14.95

*** Free book of equal or lesser value. Shipping and applicable sales tax extra.**
Cleis Press • (800) 780-2279 • orders@cleispress.com
www.cleispress.com

Rousing, Arousing Adventures with Hot Hunks

The Riddle of the Sands
By Geoffrey Knight

Will Professor Fathom's team of gay adventure-hunters uncover the legendary Riddle of the Sands in time to save one of their own? Is the Riddle a myth, a mirage, or the greatest engineering feat in the history of ancient Egypt?
"A thrill-a-page romp, a rousing, arousing adventure for queer boys-at-heart men."
—Richard Labonté, Book Marks
ISBN 978-1-57344-366-1 $14.95

Divas Las Vegas
By Rob Rosen

Filled with action and suspense, hunky blackjack dealers, divine drag queens, strange sex, and sex in strange places, plus a Federal agent or two, *Divas Las Vegas* puts the sin in Sin City.
ISBN 978-1-57344-369-2 $14.95

The Back Passage
By James Lear

Blackmail, police corruption, a dizzying network of spy holes and secret passages, and a nonstop queer orgy backstairs and everyplace else mark this hilariously hardcore mystery by a major new talent.
ISBN 978-1-57344-423-5 $13.95

The Secret Tunnel
By James Lear

"Lear's prose is vibrant and colourful...This isn't porn accompanied by a wah-wah guitar, this is porn to the strains of Beethoven's *Ode to Joy*, each vividly realised ejaculation accompanied by a fanfare and the crashing of cymbals."—*Time Out London*
ISBN 978-1-57344-329-6 $15.95

A Sticky End
A Mitch Mitchell Mystery
By James Lear

To absolve his best friend and sometimes lover from murder charges, Mitch races around London finding clues while bedding the many men eager to lend a hand—or more.
ISBN 978-1-57344-395-1 $14.95

*** Free book of equal or lesser value. Shipping and applicable sales tax extra.**
Cleis Press • (800) 780-2279 • orders@cleispress.com
www.cleispress.com

Ordering is easy! Call us toll free or fax us to place your MC/VISA order.
You can also mail the order form below with payment to:
Cleis Press, 2246 Sixth St., Berkeley, CA 94710.

ORDER FORM

QTY	TITLE	PRICE

SUBTOTAL	
SHIPPING	
SALES TAX	
TOTAL	

Add $3.95 postage/handling for the first book ordered and $1.00 for each additional book. Outside North America, please contact us for shipping rates. California residents add 9% sales tax. Payment in U.S. dollars only.

*** Free book of equal or lesser value. Shipping and applicable sales tax extra.**

Cleis Press • Phone: (800) 780-2279 • Fax: (510) 845-8001
orders@cleispress.com • www.cleispress.com
You'll find more great books on our website

Follow us on Twitter @cleispress • Friend/fan us on Facebook